Visitors, Vanishings and Va-Va-Va Voom

"Hello, Ally," Mrs Hudson replied, as I panicked. "Sorry, but Jen's not in right now – she went round to Chloe's for tea."

"Oh. Oh, OK. That's great. Thank you. *Bye!*"

I don't think I've ever been so glad to get off the phone. Well, apart from the time I phoned for a pizza and found I'd called the local police station by accident. (And no, the sergeant at the Crime Desk *didn't* laugh when I asked for a pepperoni pizza with extra cheese, please.)

It was only when I put the phone down that I realized two things: a) Fluffy had curled herself asleep in my lap without me even noticing; and b) Chloe hadn't said anything about Jen being round at hers when I spoke to her a minute ago.

Fluffy acting like a cute cat instead of a ninja warrior? Jen supposed to be somewhere she wasn't?

As Alice in Wonderland once said, curiouser and curiouser…

Available in this series:

The Past, the Present and the Loud, Loud Girl
Dates, Double Dates and Big, Big Trouble
Butterflies, Bullies and Bad, Bad Habits
Friends, Freak-Outs and Very Secret Secrets
Boys, Brothers and Jelly-Belly Dancing
Sisters, Super-Creeps and Slushy, Gushy Love Songs
Parties, Predicaments and Undercover Pets
Tattoos, Telltales and Terrible, Terrible Twins
Angels, Arguments and a Furry Merry Christmas
Mates, Mysteries and Pretty Weird Weirdness
Daisy, Dad and the Huge, Small Surprise
Rainbows, Rowan and True, True Romance(?)

And look out for:

Crushes, Cliques and the Cool School Trip
Hassles, Heart-pings! and Sad, Happy Endings

Find out more about Ally's World at
www.karenmccombie.com

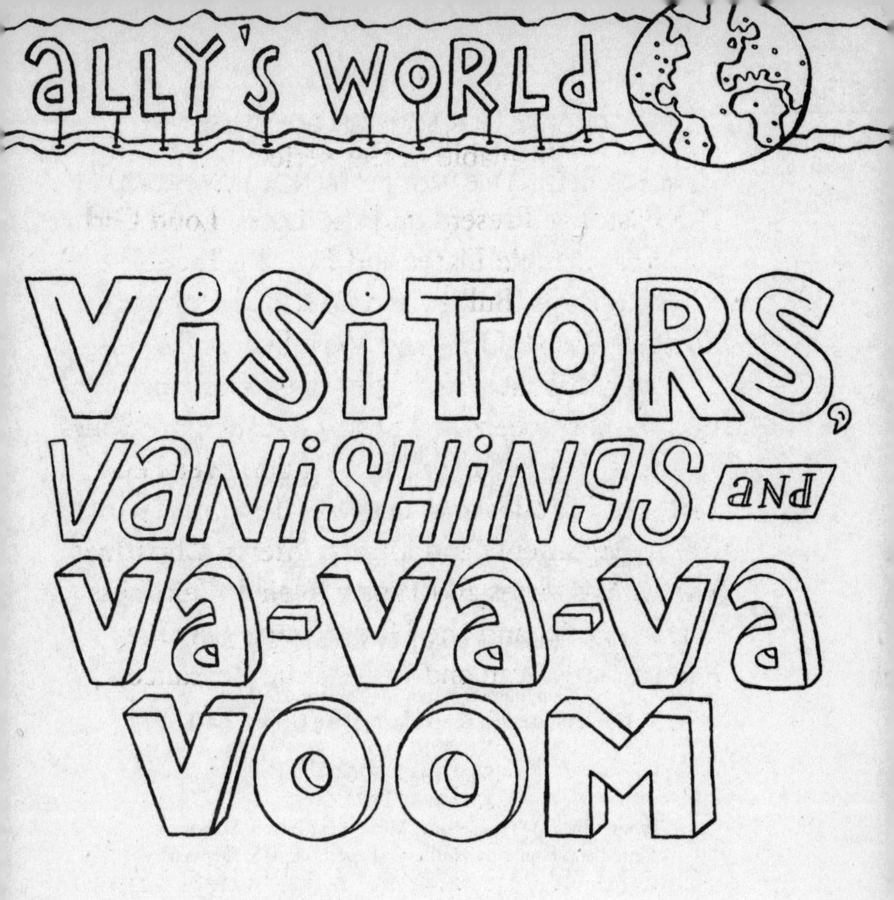

KAREN McCOMBIE

SCHOLASTIC

FOR SPIKE (FOR BEING AN ACE ARTIST
AND FOR HELPING ME WITH MY FRENCH HOMEWORK)

Scholastic Children's Books,
Commonwealth House, 1–19 New Oxford Street,
London WC1A 1NU, UK
A division of Scholastic Ltd
London ~ New York ~ Toronto ~ Sydney ~ Auckland
Mexico City ~ New Delhi ~ Hong Kong

First published in the UK by Scholastic Ltd, 2003

ISBN 0 439 98204 9

Typeset by TW Typesetting, Midsomer Norton, Somerset
Printed and bound by Nørhaven Paperback A/S, Denmark

10 9 8 7 6 5 4 3 2 1

Contents

PROLOGUE

Dear Mum,
Zut! as French people might say when they're a bit grumpy.

Thing is, you get pretty used to noise and chaos if you happen to live at 28 Palace Heights Road. But somehow, this particular Sunday, it's like living in a cross between a little kids' school playground, a noisy café, a pit stop for the Tour de France, a market in downtown Cairo and a safari park where the animals have gone doolally and are stampeding about all over the place.

That's what you get when you combine a visit by Tor's friend Freddie and some of Tor's other classmates; Billy's mum dropping by for a coffee and natter with you (Mum); Rowan's mate Chazza getting his bike repaired in the hall by Dad; Rowan and her other mate Von shimmying to a blaring belly-dance video in the living room; and three dogs and five cats racing around the house being chased by Tor, Ivy, Freddie and other small noisy

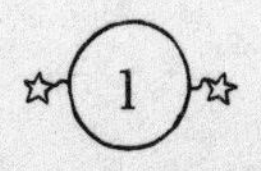

people. (No wonder Linn has barricaded herself in her room and put her Sugababes CD on *LOUD*.)

I can't copy Linn and do the same, 'cause of the *tiny* problem of my bedroom door being missing. Dad took it off to fix a broken hinge, but there must be a national shortage of hinges or something, since a couple of weeks have passed by and I *still* have a gaping hole where a useful bit of wood should be. I've managed not to let it bug me over the last few days, but when all you want to do on a Sunday is scribble quietly in your journal, you realize how useful a door is for keeping out unwanted noise/ stampeding small siblings/stampeding small siblings' friends/stampeding animals being chased by stampeding small siblings (and friends).

Ho-hum.

Thank goodness for garden sheds, that's all I can say (and I know someone *else* who'd agree with me, but more about that mysterious vanishing trick later...). Hopefully all the mayhem and madness will stay safely in the house, and no one will stampede out here and disturb me while I'm getting on with my writing in peace. Well, not *quite* in peace – I am slightly distracted by the fact that I seem to have a splinter in my bottom. That's the downside of sitting in garden sheds; they may have doors, but they don't automatically come

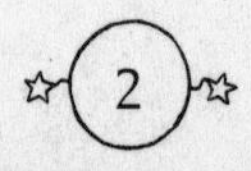

lined with feather-soft satin floor cushions. Sadly.

Speaking of feathers, Britney seems to be doing some kind of pigeon tap dance on the roof just now, which also makes concentrating kind of hard. (What's wrong with perching on tree branches, for goodness' sake?)

Still ... us authors have to suffer for our art, don't we? (Fnar!) And if I didn't put up with this hardship, and carry on writing my journal, how would the world ever know about the visitors, or the vanishings, or the "va-va-va voom"*?

Love you lots,

Ally

(your Love Child No. 3)

* French for "Oooooh, *he's* cute!", according to Kyra Davies. But you shouldn't always listen to her – after all, last week I caught her teaching Tor and Ivy how to say "Bog off"** in French.

** "*Dégage*", in case you wanted to know.

OOOOH LA LA!

So, another day, another dilemma…

Which of my two mates was going to win the current quarrel? I'd have to bet on Kyra rather than Kellie – thing is, even if Kyra's totally wrong about something, she can still happily argue her point till you surrender through sheer exhaustion/die of boredom/are on the point of strangling her with your bare hands.

"It's just not possible."

"It is too, Kyra!"

"No, it's not. It's total rubbish."

"It's not!"

"Is too."

"Is not!"

"Is too."

"Is not!"

Me, Sandie, Chloe (slowly blowing a pink bubble of gum) and Salma turned our heads from side to side as the conversation ping-ponged back and forth between our two other friends.

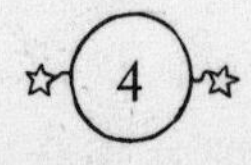

"Listen, Kellie," said Kyra wearily. "Something *that* important to your life – nobody could hide it from you."

"Could too!" Kellie replied, lamely.

"Could too!" wasn't exactly a convincing argument. Poor Kel – Kyra was in the process of trashing one of her favourite fantasies, and Kellie was powerless to stop her.

OK, so watching these two bickering had passed a few boring minutes for the rest of us while we hovered near the main school entrance this sunny Monday morning. But now it was time to rescue Kellie, before Kyra drove her loopy.

"Yeah, *right*!" I saw Kyra smirk, in that irritatingly condescending way she does so well. "Technically, there's no *way* you could be the princess of an entire sodding country and grow up not knowing anything about it!"

"Yeah," I butted in. "And *technically*, Kyra, *The Princess Diaries* was just a *film*."

A well-worn film we'd watched yesterday evening, when we were all round at Kellie's for a Girls' Video Night.

"*And* it's a book," Sandie butted in in a whisper by my side, but no one paid any attention.

"And your point *is*, Ally?" Kyra said to me archly, putting her hands on her hips, and

managing to pull her short school skirt up a few centimetres at the same time. (She did that deliberately, I was sure, 'cause a couple of half-decent boys from Rowan's year were just ambling by...)

"The point *is*, Kyra, films are allowed to use artistic licence, aren't they?" I shrugged. "Things don't happen *exactly* the way they would in real life."

"See?!" Kellie jumped in, making no more sense than she had when she'd burst out with "Could too!".

Poor Kellie had taken nothing but stick for making us sit through that film for the forty trillionth time, but it wasn't *her* fault that the brand new teen flick that Chloe had arrived with – fresh from her dad's shop – was a dud and had jammed five minutes after she'd stuck it in Kel's video player. But then, it *did* get pretty funny when we spotted Kellie mouthing along to chunks of Mia, the heroine's, dialogue. You know, I think that would be Kellie's ultimate dream ... to have some long-lost relative ship up at her council flat with a tiara and (in her version of the fairy tale) the keys to an island paradise in the Caribbean...

Whether it was directed at me or at Kellie, I *had* expected Kyra to come back with yet another sarky reply, but she didn't. All she had to say was…

"Va-va-va voom!"

"Er … *what*?" I frowned at her, and then realized Kyra had obviously got bored with arguing and was now noseying at something far more interesting going on over my shoulder.

"They're *here*!" hissed Salma excitedly, making me, Sandie and Kellie whip our heads around to see what our mates had already spotted.

"Oh, yeah – looks like our visitors have arrived!"

Don't know why Kyra put it like that. 'Cause technically, the interesting-looking, exotic-sounding strangers currently wending around the corner of the building towards us were exchange students, not "visitors". And another thing; they weren't "ours"; they were here to stay with pupils in the year above us.

"Where did *they* come from?" I mumbled, lifting my sunglasses off my nose and sticking them on the top of my head as they came closer.

"France?" Chloe suggested cheekily, blowing a big pink bubble at me.

"*Very* funny. I'm laughing *hysterically* on the inside. But I meant, how did we miss seeing their coach?"

"Pop! *A-heucchhhh!* Cuh-cuh-*cuh*!"

I think Chloe had been planning on answering me – probably with something equally cheeky but she seemed to have forgotten about the bubble she'd just blown. Somehow or other, she accidentally inhaled, popping the gum and half-choking on it instead. Wow … all that splattered pink goo was going to take *ages* to pick off.

"It must have parked around the side," Salma whispered, keeping her eyes glued to the laughing, chatting, uniform-free students that were ambling by, directed inside our school by one of our teachers, Mr Matthews.

"All right, girls?" he asked breezily, when he saw us. "You're all very punctual today!"

Um, I guess we *were* very punctual. Personally, I never *normally* come to school twenty minutes early (twenty *seconds* early is more my style), but we'd decided last night at Kellie's that it would be an ace idea to come and gawp at the coach-load of potentially cute-looking French boys who'd be arriving first thing. (OK, there were French girls there as well, but to be totally honest, I don't think I'd have left my cosy bed twenty minutes too soon just to come and see *them* show up.)

"But Mr Matthews, we're *always* here this early!" Kyra lied sweetly to our teacher.

"Yes, just like you *always* spend plenty of

quality time on your homework for me, Kyra," Mr Matthews answered her back, in a voice laden with sarcasm, before he stomped up the steps and held the door open for people to pass through.

"Oooh, look at those two with the floppy fringes!" said Kellie, with a quiet urgency, and with a nod of her head towards two distinctly cute lads.

"*'They are not from our world...'*" I mumbled in my best alien voice. Too right. No boys at Palace Gates School looked as effortlessly, hair-rufflingly drool-worthy as those two.

"Hey – they're staring at us!" said Kyra, in what I'd *like* to say was a whisper, but most certainly wasn't.

Those boys ... I really hoped their English was so lousy that they wouldn't have heard what Kyra had just come out with, but from the grins that instantly lit up their faces, I guessed they were pretty fluent. (Rats.)

"*Dis-donc, celles-la sont pas mals!*" I heard one of them say, blatantly pointing in our direction.

"*Surtout elle aux grands yeux bleus!*" the other one chipped in, as the two of them slipped by us and were ushered inside by Mr Matthews.

"What did they say! *What did they say?!*" asked Chloe, spinning around to us, all wide eyes and splotches of pink gum still stuck on her chin.

This is where we needed Jen – we all did French

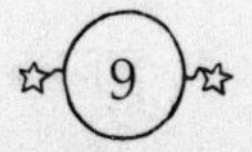

classes, but we were truly terrible at it (just ask Mr Matthews), apart from Jen. But then – weirdly – Jen hadn't turned up this morning (just like she hadn't turned up for the Girls' Video Night last night), even though we'd left her a message telling her what we were planning.

"I think the first boy said something about us not being bad!" said Sandie excitedly.

"And then the other lad said, 'Specially the one with' –"

"The one with *what*?" Kyra asked agitatedly, frustrated at the way Salma had just started and then stopped with a frown.

Maybe Kyra was hoping it was "the one with the short skirt", but I was fairly sure that wasn't the case. 'Cause *I'd* caught the last part, even if nobody else had...

" 'Especially the one ... with the big blue eyes!' " I blurted out.

And the one with the big blue eyes certainly – sadly – wasn't me (mine are brown), or Kyra (ditto), or Kellie (ditto ditto), or Salma (ditto ditto ditto), or Chloe (green).

"Oh ... my ... God!" Kellie gasped on behalf of us all, as we turned to gape at a stunned, pink-cheeked Sandie, who was staring back at us with her saucer-sized, baby-blue eyes.

Good grief – Sandie couldn't have been more gobsmacked if someone had told her she was the blimmin' Princess of Genovia...

It was like sitting next to a radioactive lump of metal.

Sandie was positively *glowing* next to me in assembly, partly through sheer surprised pleasure and partly through sheer embarrassment. When you're one of the shyest girls in the western hemisphere, I guess it's very, *very* hard to take a compliment, specially when there are boys involved.

"Is she OK, Ally?" Kellie whispered in my ear, nudging her head in Sandie's direction.

"Think she's in shock, like car crash victims," I mumbled back.

Maybe my best friend needed ... what was it called again? That rotten-egg-scented stuff Victorian ladies were always sniffing at when their corsets were fastened so tight they were in danger of fainting? Oh, yeah; *smelling* salts. Or maybe a slap around the face would have brought her back to her senses; they do that all the time in old black-and-white movies when someone's losing it. ("For God's sake, Mildred, pull yourself together!" *Whack!* "Oh, thank you, Arthur! I feel so much better now!")

Hmmm. I didn't have any smelling salts handy (or rotten eggs), and I liked Sandie too much to slap her, so I'd just have to let her sit and glow with shock at the very idea that someone (a cute FRENCH someone, to be accurate) could fancy shy little her more than skinny, pretty Kyra or glam, gorgeous Salma, never mind Chloe or Kellie, or even ordinary old me. I mean, Sandie was still stupefied by the fact that she had somehow, magically, managed to get herself a boyfriend (i.e. Billy).

To be honest, as far as the compliment went, I was quietly chuffed for Sandie, *and* it was one in the eye for Kyra, who always thought she was irresistible to anyone in trousers and bumfluff...

Just as our headteacher, Mr Bashir, appeared on the stage and all the teachers started shushing us into silence (ha! Fat chance!), I sneaked a quick sideways look at Sandie's luminously flushed face ... and just beyond her, I couldn't help noticing that Kyra seemed to be doing an impression of a meerkat. At first I thought she was watching Jen, who – along with another couple of late arrivals – was scurrying into the hall. But no; I could suddenly tell that she was stretching her already long neck so she could get a better ogle at the French kids, who'd all been herded into rows of seats in the far corner of the hall.

"Morning, boys and girls!" Mr Bashir boomed jovially.

"Morning, Mr Bashir!" we all droned back in unison. Everyone except Chloe, next to me, who was busy doodling something on a bit of paper.

Out of the corner of my eye I could make out Jen slithering into the seat Salma had kept for her. I wiggled my fingers in a wave "hello", but she couldn't have noticed, 'cause she didn't smile or wave back.

"Well, it's good to look around and see so many alert, wide-awake faces this Monday morning!" Mr Bashir joked, in that way that teachers do (i.e. what they've said is not *actually* funny). "Anyway, without further ado, I'd like to welcome some new faces to the school, all the way from the small Normandy town of..."

I completely missed which small Normandy town the French kids were from, because Chloe was digging me in the ribs with her surprisingly pointy elbow and "pssssst!"ing at me.

"Check it out!" she whispered, passing me a piece of paper with her scrawled handwriting on it. "Pass it on!"

I focused on the scrawl: "*DARE!!*", it announced at the top of the page, with underlining so hard it nearly went through the paper. *"This week, each of*

us HAS to talk to a French boy, a) in FRENCH!, and b) with at least ONE of the rest of us there to witness it! Last one to do The Dare is a big, hairy maggot!!!"

Well, I definitely didn't fancy being a hairy maggot. (Whatever one of those is.)

And hey, this Dare thing could be fun – specially in a week when the two "highlights" of school were going to be a teeth-grittingly scary maths test and a scheduled talk from the school nurse about the importance of personal hygiene. (Double yuck! or whatever the French equivalent might be…)

Chapter 2

"IF YOU'RE HAPPY AND YOU KNOW IT, PAT A DOG..."

Squelch, squeat! Squelch, squeat! Squelch...

What a difference a few hours can make.

Yep, at 8.30 a.m., the sky had been Mediterranean blue, the sun had pretended it was July instead of late September, and I'd hurried to school *minus* my blazer and *plus* a pair of v. cool shades (free with a copy of *Sugar* magazine back at the start of summer).

Who'd have guessed that by lunchtime, a particularly *mean* bunch of rain clouds would swoop along, chucking down water so hard I looked like I'd just gone for a fully clothed dip in the Thames by the time I made it home? As for my shoes, it sounded as if I was treading on soggy, indignant mice with every step. *Squelch, squeat! Squelch, squeat! Squelch...*

The weather wasn't the *only* thing that had changed for the mega-worse over the course of the morning. My mind (which, let's face it, is not exactly a reliable organ), had done a complete swivel on the matter of The Dare. I mean, who had I been kidding when I first read Chloe's note in assembly? Trying to strike up a conversation with one of the French boys, with *my* terrible French accent? I don't *think* so. I'd probably end up asking them a harmless question like "Are you enjoying being in London?" and it would come out as "Do you like stroking artichokes?" or something just as freakily *wrong*, and I'd end up being not only the laughing stock of *my* school, but the laughing stock of some school in the small Normandy town of Whatever-it's-called too.

And, I realized, as I pushed the garden gate open with one dripping hand, there was no *way* I could get out of The Dare – Chloe and the rest of them would never let me off the hook, not if *they* were all game for it. Unless ... unless, of course, I developed a hideous illness that meant I had to stay in bed all week, until the French kids were safely back on their coach next Monday morning. Ace idea! Only it meant I had about fifteen seconds in-between walking up the path and opening the front door to come up with an illness convincing enough for Mum to order me to bed and make me stay there with only a pile of magazines, a huge mug of hot chocolate and a random pet or two for company. (Bliss...)

It's got to be something to do with getting soaked, I thought, as I *squelch-squeat*ed my way up the garden path.

A dusty part of my brain whirred into action, inputting the keywords "Damp+cold+germs", and immediately – well, as quick as a computer that's filled with fluff and biscuit crumbs – words came flooding into my head: flu; pneumonia; *double* pneumonia; pleurisy; bronchitis; tuberculosis; consumption; dry rot...

Before I could settle on anything in particular and develop instant symptoms, two quite spooky things happened – the rain clouds did a disappearing act, as if God had suddenly flipped a light switch, and our front door flew open just as my hand reached out to grab the chunky wooden doorknob.

"Saw you coming up the road – isn't the weather weird?" Mum smiled happily, gazing up at the now sun-filled sky as she began towelling my hair dry on the front step. "I mean weird in a *good* way."

The weather wasn't the only thing that was weird in a good way. Having Mum back home – *properly* this time – definitely fitted into that weird/good category. And the fact that Mum and Dad were all twinkly-eyed and loved-up with each other was pretty weird/good too. It had only been a week since we'd all gone to Cornwall to find Mum and Ivy after that whole misunderstanding when they'd first turned up at Grandma's wedding, but time had done this weird/good trick of making it seem much longer; almost as if those four years Mum had been gone were just a bad dream; almost as if we'd *always* had a little sister called Ivy kicking around. It's like lunchtimes during the week; up until recently – while Linn hung out in the school dinner hall with her Sixth Form cronies, and Tor dived into his Spiderman tuckbox at *his* school – me and Rowan both mooched about at home, with only Radio One, Aussie soaps, boring/inedible sandwiches and scavenging pets for company. Now, there was Mum to chat to, Ivy's latest (blobby) drawings to inspect, and even *more* scavenging pets milling around (Mum and Ivy's dog Ben had joined the zoo at our house). And it was brilliant – specially when there was a bowl of Mum's home-made soup waiting for us instead of "me"-made skanky sandwiches. Oh yes, it was *all* so brilliantly weird/good that I couldn't help grinning at Mum through the towel and my mussed-up hair as we bumbled into the house together, somehow managing to shut the front door behind us. Good grief; I was *way* too blissed-out to fake symptoms of sneezily diseases *now*.

"Ally! A game! C'*mon*!" chirruped a teeny-tiny voice, as a small hand grabbed mine and started hauling me down the hall in the direction of the kitchen.

"Ivy, your sister's soaking wet! She needs to go and get changed before she catches a chill!" Mum tried to explain.

"Don't worry – I'll get changed in a minute," I reassured her, as I felt myself being yanked forward in determined lurches.

In her pink dungarees and strawberry hair bobbles, Ivy may have *looked* like a cute, sweet three-and-a-half-year-old kid, but with a tug that strong, it wouldn't have surprised me to find out she'd been reincarnated from a *buffalo*.

"Fine," Mum called after me, as I gave in and let myself be dragged through the kitchen and out of the back door into the blaze of newly returned sunshine. "Anyway, food'll be ready in about five minutes. I've had to put on more since we've got an extra mouth to feed!"

I wondered what she was on about for a micro-second or two, but the sudden brightness of the light outside in the garden was positively eyeball-melting, and I was too busy trying to wrestle my freebie sunshades from the top of my head, where they were tangled in damp twirls of hair, to care.

"So – *ow* ! – what game do you want to play?" I asked Ivy, wincing as the sunglasses tugged at my tangles. (At this rate I was going to go back to school in the afternoon minus several chunks of hair. Well, at least I'd have *something* to chat about for The Dare. I'd just have to get Mr Matthews to tell me what "Hi – wanna see my bald patches?" was in French first...)

"Singin' game!" Ivy informed me earnestly, standing on our wet, scruffy lawn in her pink plastic sandals.

Also on the lawn, Rolf and Winslet (our wet, scruffy dogs) and their new doggy buddy Ben the golden retriever, were padding around and sniffing like crazy, as if the recent shower of rain contained a million secret smelly messages for them to inhale and decode. Meanwhile, a line of sunbathing cats watched the mutts in a superior, serene way from the garden wall. Colin and three cats who weren't Colin (Eddie, Frankie and Derek it seemed from the shortness of their black and white coats) had been joined by Tabitha, the elderly Persian cat from next door, and all five of them were curled up, paws tucked under, smiling identical smug catty smiles as the sun gently toasted their fur.

"What sort of singing game?" I asked Ivy, a final yank freeing my glasses.

"'*If you're happy and you know it, clap your hands!*'" a voice began trilling just behind me, and I whirled around to find Rowan – and Alfie! – perching their bums on the windowsill of the utility room.

"Oh!" I mumbled in embarrassed surprise. (You might guess here that it wasn't *Rowan* who I was surprised to see. And you might *also* guess that – no matter how much I'd tried to convince myself that I was over him since he'd started dating my sister – I *still* had a crush as big as Bavaria on Alfie...)

And right now he looked as embarrassed as me, with Rowan nudging him with her elbow, forcing him to join in (a little limply, I noticed) with the clapping. He seemed to be drawing the line at singing though – all he managed was a quick face twitch in my direction that was halfway between a hello grin and a look of pure humiliation.

"Sing!" Ivy instructed me, clapping her chubby doll-sized hands together.

"Yeah, come on, Ally!" Rowan giggled. "She's been making us do this for the last ten minutes. Don't see why you should get off doing it!"

And because I didn't have a clue what else to say or do in front of Alfie, I did as my sisters told me, and joined in a few verses of this stupid song that I hadn't sung since Tor was tiny. At first – especially since I knew Alfie had to have witnessed the ungraceful hair-tugging moment back there – I was so self-conscious I wanted the ground to open up so deep that me and my sunglasses would end up in Australia. But after about seventeen verses that were getting steadily sillier and sillier, I have to say we were all having pretty good fun, and by the time I'd suggested "If you're happy and you know it, pat a dog", I seemed to have managed to forget to be shy in front of Alfie *or* stressed out by the idea of looking like a goofball doing Chloe's Dare. Well, it's very hard to stay stressed when you're all running around the lawn, chasing dogs that won't stay still to get patted, and practically falling over, you're laughing so much.

Then I felt it; it was as if one of those pesky, mean-tempered clouds had slithered over the sun again. But no – the sun was still shining, with nothing much in the sky to disturb it apart from a swirling starling or two. The reason for the sudden drop in temperature and the invisible shadow that we all somehow felt was standing in the kitchen doorway, with her arms folded across her crisp, white shirt.

"Linn! Sing!" announced Ivy, skipping towards our big sister.

"Not just now, sweetpea," Linn muttered gently, while firing death-ray glares over the top of Ivy's head at Rowan and Alfie.

"You *never* come home at lunchtime!" Rowan blurted out, twirling a finger nervously around one of the myriad of tiny plaits dangling from her head today.

No wonder Ro was nervous. Maybe I wasn't too thrilled that my sister and my dream boy had started dating, but Linn had really taken it badly. OK, so maybe she had given up ranting at Rowan about it, but for the last week she'd changed tactics and chosen to blank our mad middle sister instead, which I guess proved that she still hadn't *quite* forgiven Ro for going out with her best mate.

"I forgot an essay I have to hand in this afternoon," Linn answered Rowan curtly, while looking straight at Alfie. "So ... what are you doing here?"

"Alfie's just popped round to see Rowan, and he's staying for lunch," came Mum's cheerful voice, as she appeared in the kitchen doorway behind Linn, before disappearing again and clattering the lid of some pot or other.

"We're still seeing each other tonight, right?" Linn directed a statement, rather than a question, at Alfie.

"Yeah! Yeah, of course!" he bumbled awkwardly.

"Right – soup's ready, folks!" Mum called out of the open kitchen window.

"Don't put out any for me – I'm going back to school," said Linn, turning on her heel and walking, stern-faced, back into the house.

"Oh, OK..." I heard Mum answer her, as Linn's footsteps snip-snapped across the red tiles of the kitchen floor.

At first, I thought the high-pitched howl might have come from Rowan, growling out her frustration at Linn. But that wasn't really Ro's style (she's more of a hiccuping sobber), and she certainly didn't *hiss*.

"Fluffy! *Noooooooo!*" I yelped, as I caught sight of a long-haired cat that wasn't Colin launch itself from the cover of an overgrown bush, run perpendicularly up the wall and batter the daylights out of poor, unsuspecting Tabitha, much to the surprise of a dozy Colin and co.

Without stopping to think, I sprinted over and lunged for Fluffy, before she raced over the wall after the speedily fleeing white moggy.

"*Hssssssssssssssssss...*" Fluffy snarled, her four fat, furry paws scrabbling in thin air as she struggled to get free.

Ooops ... from the clumps of pure white hair

wedged in her claws, it seemed like I wasn't the only one to end up with bald patches today.

"What's your problem with poor old Tabitha?" Rowan cooed at our still-hissing cat.

"Maybe she doesn't like another female on her turf," Mum suggested, as she came over with a worried-looking Ivy clutching her hand.

It was only when Alfie reached over and stroked Fluffy's head that her beautiful slanted eyes lost that glimmer of hate-filled fury and she started to purr.

Hmm – now *who* did this bundle of catty bad temper suddenly remind me of…?

DRONGO ALERT!

"Now, girls – compare and contrast…" said Chloe, putting on the snooty, authoritative voice our science teacher Miss Kyriacou sometimes uses when she's trying to come over like a proper teacher (it doesn't fool *us*).

It was afternoon break on Monday afternoon, we were outside in the sunshine and Chloe was holding her arms outstretched, pointing in two different directions. Over in the red corner (i.e. by the gym), a bunch of lads were roaring and laughing as one of them swung a shoe by the laces, aiming for the roof of the gym presumably, while another lad – who was hopping around in a solo matching shoe – tried to make a grab for it but was being held back by yet more roaring, laughing lads. In the blue corner (i.e. over by the railings), a bunch of the French boys who'd arrived this morning were smiling and chatting with the adoring female fans (French and Crouch End-ish) who were currently surrounding them on all sides.

Talk about a culture clash...

"What a bunch of drongos," Kyra sighed, speaking for us all as she blinked over at the shoe-shotputter and his brain-dead mates.

"Shouldn't somebody help...?" Sandie suggested vaguely, furrowing a few lines in her forehead as she stared at the hopping boy's dilemma.

"I wouldn't if I was you," I told her. "Not unless you want to be the next person with a shoe on the roof."

Sandie automatically looked down at her new black leather mules and took one cautious step back behind me and Jen.

"Wish there was some way to hang out with *them*..." Salma sighed, tucking a strand of her long dark hair behind one neat little ear, and switching her gaze from the Palace Gates drongo contingent to the super-cool, super-laidback French boys.

I mean, to be fair, maybe the French boys were just on their best behaviour, and back home at their school in the small Normandy town of Whatever-it's-called they were just as prone to general blokey pranks that involved doing dumb things on a regular basis. And maybe the dopey lads from our school would immediately drop the drongo act if they were in a foreign country on an

exchange trip and do their best to impress the local girls with their British hipness.

"*Whaaaaaarrrrghhhhhhh…!!!*"

And then again, maybe not. The huddle of French girls over by the side entrance to the school looked *well* unimpressed by the "special" greeting they'd just received from Ben Middleton, one of our school's star morons. (What a title to be proud of!)

"Why does he always have to *moon* at everyone?" said Kellie, wrinkling up her dark brown nose at the thankfully distant sight of Ben Middleton's spotty white botty.

"Because that's obviously where he keeps his brains," Kyra snarled in disgust, which immediately cracked the rest of us up.

All of us, I noticed, except Jen.

Now what was funny (as in funny peculiar and not funny ha-ha) was that I hadn't seen Jen smile all day. Or *talk* for that matter. She hadn't talked in class (not a big surprise, seeing as teachers tend to disapprove of that sort of thing), and she hadn't talked at morning break. I knew she hadn't hung out with the others at school dinner, 'cause I'd seen her zooming out the school gates in the rain just as I'd headed home for lunch and family stress (thanks to Linn, Rowan and Fluffy…). Another

thing; we'd all been so wrapped up in the new school visitors that none of us had remembered to ask her why she hadn't turned up at Kellie's last night.

Speaking of Kellie…

"Y'know, I *could* try and find out where they're all going to be hanging out after school this week!" I heard her suddenly suggest.

Kellie's fun and friendly and nice, and 'cause she's fun and friendly and nice, people tend to blab stuff to her that they probably shouldn't blab. This makes her a most excellent gossip guru. If *she* couldn't find out where the French kids would be hanging out, not even the FBI could.

"Excellent!" Chloe enthused, clapping her hands together. "It would be a lot easier if we could trail 'em *out* of school!"

"Easier how?" Sandie blinked her blue eyes at Chloe.

"Easier to get talking to them! Easier to do The Dare, of course!"

Beside me, I sensed Sandie quiver. Yep, she was as spaced out as me at the idea of striking up a conversation with a stranger in a foreign language we were hopeless at. Actually, I wouldn't have been surprised if she phoned up with a bad case of *triple* pneumonia in the next few days…

"Brilliant!" Kyra grinned wickedly. "We'll be like detectives – following their every move!"

"*Stalkers*, you mean..." I mumbled, unconvinced.

"Oh, come on, Al!" Salma tried to cajole me. "Lighten up! It's just a laugh!"

"Until we get arrested under the anti-stalking laws!" I pointed out.

I was being serious, but luckily, everyone presumed I was joking and started laughing, which I guess stopped them suspecting I was the wuss I really am deep down.

Er, when I say, *everyone* was laughing, that didn't include Jen... Instead, she was staring down at her shoes, her fair-ish bobbed hair swinging as she kicked at an imaginary stone.

"Hey, Jen – what's up with you?" Chloe asked bluntly, spotting what I already had.

"Nothing," Jen mumbled, not even bothering to raise her gaze from the ground.

At a bit of a loss, for half a second or so, none of us said anything. And then Kellie spoke.

"I know what *you* need..." she said out loud to Jen, before glancing round at the rest of us with a conspiratorial twinkle in her eye and mouthing something slowly.

"Death By Tickling!"; that's what Kellie mouthed, and that's immediately what we did, all

leaping on Jen at once and tickling her till we got what we wanted from her – a laugh, at last.

And that one laugh told us everything we needed to know, specially since she slapped her hand over her mouth the instant the laugh had been forced out of her.

"A brace? You've got a *brace*?!" said Chloe, swapping her own grin for a frown.

Jen nodded, keeping her hand in place, and her brace under cover.

"When did you get that?" asked Salma.

Above her white-knuckled hand, Jen's tiny, button eyes were ringed with dark circles.

"Sahurday mawnin'," came her muffled reply.

"You got your brace on Saturday morning?!" Sandie repeated, just to make sure we'd heard her properly.

Jen nodded, her hair bobbing at her jawline.

"Why are you hiding it? Why didn't you tell us?" said Salma.

"'Cause I hate it."

Uh-oh … were those tears in Jen's eyes?

"Is that why you didn't come to mine last night?" Kellie checked with her.

Another wordless nod.

"So you got a brace," Kyra shrugged. "What's the big deal?"

Kyra's not the sort of person you can expect much sympathy from, but right now, I was kind of glad she'd put it so bluntly. There was no reason for Jen to be stressed out about a stupid brace. It was nothing to be embarrassed about. After all, it wasn't like her dentist had ordered her to dress as a clown for six months or something; it was only a teeny-tiny strip of wire across a few teeth.

Jen shrugged in response to Kyra, and kept her hand where it was.

"Ah, come on, Jen – let's see it!" Chloe insisted, grabbing hold of Jen's wrist and pulling it down. "I had to wear one for the whole of Year Seven, remember!"

"Yeah, come on, Jen – it's only us!" Salma urged her.

Grudgingly, slowly, Jen opened her mouth and bared her teeth.

"It's *minuscule*!" Chloe burst out. "Did you see the thing I had to wear? It was like having a stair-gate fitted to your teeth! But that – that's *nothing*. It's practically invisible!"

"It is!" I joined in, telling the truth. You'd have to be practically in snogging distance to see Jen's brace. Maybe that's what was getting to her – maybe she'd hoped by some miracle to land herself

a drop-dead droolsome French boy and now she'd ruined her chances or something.

"*Loads* of famous people have had braces!" Sandie chipped in, with her own nugget of comfort. "Like Tom Cruise, and – and—"

Jen, normally the giggliest one of the lot of us, blinked wetly at Sandie and looked like she was on the verge of a full-scale blubbathon. But school bells have no respect for people's feelings, and ours trilled loudly at that point, ordering us all back to another hour or two's torture at the hands of our teachers.

"Don't worry, Jen – it'll be all right," I tried to console her, putting my arm around her shoulders as we filed in through the main door.

"I don't *think* so..." I could just make out her mumbling above the noise and crush of everyone around us.

It didn't look like our Jen was going to be back to her giggling self any time soon. *Quel dommage*...

ROWAN, ME AND OUR BIG FAT MOUTHS

"What's that?" I asked, pointing at Cilla the rabbit, whose long teeth were making short work of the carrot Tor had given her a minute ago.

"Nooo-nooo," said Ivy, clutching her one-eared pink teddy as well as a large lettuce to her chest.

"Er, no ... that's a '*lapin*'. Can you say '*lapin*', Ivy?"

"Nooo-nooo."

"Um ... OK – what about *that*? Can you remember the name I taught you?"

I pointed at Ozzy the guinea pig who looked nervously at us both – I think he was worried that we were planning on stealing his chunk of apple or something.

"Nooo-nooo."

"No ... that's not a noo-noo," I said gently. "That's a '*cochon d'inde*'. That's the French word for 'guinea pig'."

"Nooo-nooo," said Ivy, pulling a leaf off the lettuce she was holding. I had to stop her before she made Ozzy's day and tried to stuff the whole

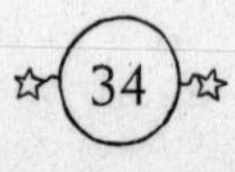

lettuce in the cage and keep just the leaf for herself.

"Nope ... we have to save some of this for their breakfast tomorrow, don't we?" I smiled at her, pulling the lettuce out and closing the hutch door on Cilla and Ozzy.

Ivy had got right into the whole routine of feeding the pets, even though she was sometimes a little over-enthusiastic. (Tor caught her throwing jam doughnuts to Britney, our pet pigeon, the other day. Grandma had just brought the doughnuts round as a treat and might have been a bit put out to find they were being treated as bird food, but me and Tor brushed the blades of grass off them and put them back on the plate in the kitchen before she noticed. Luckily Britney didn't get a chance to put any telltale peck-marks in them...)

"Oh, look! It's Rolf!" I exclaimed, as our pooch ambled up and started sniffing at the lettuce leaf clutched in Ivy's hand. He gave it a hopeful nibble, but as it wasn't dog-food-flavoured he seemed relatively unimpressed. "Can you remember what doggies say in French, Ivy?"

"Nooo-nooo," she replied brightly, bouncing the pink teddy up on to Rolf's neck. Rolf didn't bat a hairy eyelid – in fact he just yawned, letting a whiff of meaty doggy chunks waft out of his mouth. (*Yueeeewwww.*)

"*No,*" I tried to explain patiently. "In French, doggies say, '*oua, oua*'!"

So much for my not-very-serious plans* to make my kid sister a child genius by getting her into another language so young. I'd thought she'd got the hang of the few words I'd been teaching her and Tor just now, but all she was doing was *babbling* in reply.

(*I'd only started ten minutes ago.)

"She's saying 'teddy' in French," Tor informed me, coming out of the garden shed with a bundle of straw bedding in his arms.

"Huh?" I frowned at him.

"'*Nounour*' is French for 'teddy'. It was on some children's programme on TV today," my little bruv explained.

"Nooo-nooo!" Ivy repeated, bouncing her teddy off of Rolf and squishing him into my face. "Kiss nooo-nooo, Ally!"

"Ivy, tell Ally the other thing they said on the TV!" Tor encouraged her.

"Espas don-dooo-ee!" Ivy trilled happily at me, as I pretended to kiss her toy.

"What's that mean?" I checked with Tor.

"'Silly sausage.'"

Espèce d'andouille; silly sausage – that was me. Good grief, maybe we *did* have a child genius in

the family. At this rate, Ivy would stand a better chance of doing The Dare by the end of the week than *I* would…

"Hey – what's up with Tabitha's nose?"

We didn't need to turn round to know that the voice that had just spoken belonged to Rowan. Instead, me, Tor and Ivy automatically glanced up at Tabitha's normal vantage point, i.e. perched on top of the wall that separated her garden from ours.

"It's bleeding!" Tor squeaked in alarm.

"Oh, it's just a scratch!" I tried to say casually, although the vivid red slash on sweet old Tabitha's pink nose made her look like she'd been attacked by the cat equivalent of Zorro. "She had a bit of a fight with Fluffy at lunchtime. Didn't she, Rowan? It must have happened then."

"*Fluffy* did *that*?" Tor asked me, a look of pained confusion on his seven-year-old face. "But why would she hurt Tabitha?"

Tor is mad to the point of *insane* about animals. The thing is, he's still too young to get his head around the fact that life isn't all squeaky toys and tickles under the chin for our furry, feathery or scaly friends. In his rose-tinted version of the animal kingdom, lions eat pizza, sparrowhawks hunt dandelions, and none of our pet cats would *ever* lay a claw on a fellow cat.

"I think Fluffy's just a bit grumpy with Tabitha for sitting on her space on the wall," I explained, simplifying things as best as I could. "It's like a territory thing."

"I know how Tabitha feels," Rowan grumbled, rubbing an imaginary scratch on her nose as she ambled over to us in a tight turquoise vest top and over-sized men's dungarees, with her bare toes peeking out from under the layered folds of denim. With her mini-braids scooped up into a ponytail high on her head, altogether she looked like a cross between a little kid, a plumber and a pineapple.

"What do you mean?" I asked her, taking the bag of old straw bedding from Tor and heading over to the compost heap (posh name for the pile of rubbish mouldering away at the back of the garden).

"It's ... it's *nous soeur*," said Rowan hesitantly, as she trailed me over the lawn.

Aha – it seemed like me and Ro were about to have a conversation in code, which we often lapse into when we don't want Tor knowing what we're yakking about. But don't go thinking we have some amazing, ground-breaking, spy-style system for our coded conversations – oh no. One of us will just start babbling something ridiculous (e.g. "Ooh, Ally! Why don't you, me and Tor go to the

window and look at the moon, right *now*!") and hope that the other one catches on (i.e. realizes that translates as, "Eek – I've just remembered that there's a big nudie scene coming up in this film and I don't fancy explaining to Tor what's going on!").

Today – kind of appropriately in the circumstances – it seemed that Rowan had chosen to tell me what she had to say *en Français*.

"Huh? Which *soeur*?"

OK, make that Franglais. I had a feeling this chat we were about to have wouldn't score me very high marks in a French oral exam...

"What do you mean, 'which *soeur*'?"

I think Rowan was forgetting that we had more than one *soeur* these days.

"*Grande ou petite*?" I asked her, as I up-ended the bag and shook the smelly straw out on to the grassy heap.

"*Grande, naturellement!*" stated Rowan, slipping her hands behind the bib of her dungarees.

Well, I kind of *knew* the subject for discussion would be Linn, as anyone with the IQ of a cucumber could guess.

"*Qu'est-ce que c'est?*"

"It's just Linn ... *quel râleuse*!"

"She's what?"

Remember, Rowan's two years ahead of me at school – her vocabulary was obviously a lot better than mine.

"A 'misery-guts'," Ro explained.

"Well, *c'est vrai,*" I shrugged in agreement.

After all, going in a major huffle-puffle over your best friend dating your sister is all very well when you first find out, but carrying on with it was just plain dumb. I mean, it wasn't even as if Linn fancied Alfie or anything (the fool!).

"*J'en ai ras le bol...*" Rowan sighed, kicking at an innocent daisy with a bare toe.

"You what?" I had to check with her again for a translation. (I noticed she had now slid her elbows inside her dungarees. Was she making like a snail? Was her head going to disappear inside her denim shell next?)

"I'm fed up!" she repeated, in a language I could understand a little better. "*Pourquoi Linn est-elle toujours si mesquine?*"

Right, I was pretty sure I understood that: "*mesquine*" meant "mean" and no, I didn't understand why Linn always had to be mean.

"Why are you talking about Linn?" Tor's voice suddenly asked, right beside us.

Me and Rowan stared down at him, and then at each other – pink-cheeked at having been caught

gossiping (half) in another language – then back at him again.

"How did you know we were talking about Linn? We were speaking in French!" Rowan frowned at him, as she struggled to wriggle her arms free from inside her dungarees (it looked like it had been easier going in than getting out).

"Yeah, I didn't understand the French bits. Just the bits when you said 'Linn'…"

So much for our coded conversation. There was definitely a flaw in it, I could see that now…

"We're just fooling around," I laughed, unconvincingly. "Ooh, look – is Ivy meant to be feeding straw to Rolf?"

Quick as a small flash, Tor was off to rescue our dumb dog, who'll try (to eat) anything once. And then throw it up if he doesn't like it.

"Look, why don't you get Alfie to speak to her about how she's behaving?" I suggested, in English, now that Tor was preoccupied and out of earshot. I didn't bother suggesting that Rowan spoke to Linn about her behaviour – that would be like telling a baby gazelle to go lick a tiger.

"He wants to do that, but I told him not to!" she gushed, her eyes wide with alarm.

"Why?"

Rowan's dead sweet, but she does have a brain full of fluff, glitter and airy emptiness, so it can be difficult to work out what she's getting at.

"She might think I've put him up to it, which will make her more cross with me. Or – even if Linn *doesn't* think I put him up to it – she might fall out with him anyway, and then me and him being together would bug her even more. So either way—"

"—she's going to be mad at you," I finished off Ro's sentence for her.

"Exactly. God, you're so good at understanding stuff, Ally! You really are!"

I couldn't help smiling – compliments are always nice to get, even if they make your toes curl a bit.

"And … and that's why I thought it might be a good idea if *you* spoke to Linn about how she's acting!"

Aha … so, *that's* what the compliment was for.

"Rowan, I would love to talk to Linn for you," I began to tell my sister, straightfaced.

"Really?" Rowan gasped, clapping her hands together.

"Yes," I nodded. "My only condition is that I will need half a million pounds, extensive plastic surgery and a forged passport so I can take up my new identity in a foreign country *after* Linn threatens to kill me."

"How about five quid and I do all your chores for a month?" Rowan suggested lamely.

"How about we just keep our fingers crossed that Linn gets bored of sulking soon?" I suggested instead.

"Hu-*ruff* ... hu-*rufff*..." grumbled Rolf in the background as he threw up a bundle of hamster bedding...

KYRA DARES TO DO THE DARE

"What are you having, Ally?"

"Er, boiled shoe in a light mud gravy, I think," I replied to Salma's question as I peered at the scraggy piece of meat flopped beside a pile of soggy chips.

This was a bad idea. This was why I didn't stay for school dinners. This was all Sandie's idea.

"We should do it, Ally!" she'd tried to persuade me when we'd bumped into each other on the way to school this morning. "Kellie says all the French students are staying for lunch. It'll be fun to hang out with them—"

"*Near* them," I corrected her.

"OK, *near* them, and maybe we'd get a chance to do The Dare!"

Sandie seemed a bit bright-eyed and bushy-tailed about The Dare all of a sudden. I'd thought she'd be even more nervous than me about doing it.

"What, you think you might strike up a

conversation with one of the French boys over the mushy peas or something?"

"Who said anything about a conversation?" Sandie had blinked at me. "I was thinking that maybe I could just say, '*Excusez-moi!*' to one of them in the dinner queue, and then that would be my dare done!"

"You really think Chloe's going to let you off with just saying '*excusez-moi*' to someone?!" I'd quizzed her dubiously.

"Well, yeah – she'll *have* to! She didn't say anything about how *long* you had to talk to them; just that it had to be in French, and one of the rest of us had to witness it!"

You know, Sandie had obviously given this a lot of thought, and she was right. Good grief, it was an excellent plan – one simple "*excusez-moi*" or "*merci beaucoup*" if one of the French boys moved out of the way for me and the whole Dare was done, and Chloe and the rest of them couldn't say a thing!

It was just a pity I had to suffer the so-called food here. It was also a pity that all the exchange students seemed to have arrived early and were already sitting down eating their boiled shoe in gravy or whatever by the time we arrived, so bang went any chance of bumping into them by the cutlery trays. (Drat...)

"Is this shepherd's pie *soup*?!" asked Kyra, holding up a forkful of lumpy brown gloop and watching it drip through the prongs. "Wish I'd got the quiche instead."

"No, you don't," said Kellie, poking around in the middle of her slab of quiche like she was dissecting it.

"Why?" asked Sandie. "What's wrong with it?"

"It's made of egg."

"Duh...!" droned Salma. "We all know that! But what else is in it?"

"More egg," moaned Kellie. "They seem to have forgotten to put anything else in there..."

After a moment's consultation, I was just swapping my boiled shoe for Kellie's egg-and-egg quiche (seemed the lesser of two inedible evils) when Chloe suddenly shushed us.

"OK – shut up about the food, you lot," she ordered, glancing round the table at us all – which wasn't totally fair since Jen was silently swirling strands of spaghetti around her plate (and not eating much of it, I noticed). "Aren't we forgetting something?"

"Like?" suggested Kyra, pushing her plate away in disgust.

"Like no one's done The Dare, yet!"

Chloe banged on the table with the dull end of

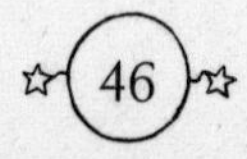

her knife, to underline her point.

"Chill out, Chloe – we've got all week!" Salma shrugged.

"And the weekend!" Kellie chipped in. "They always have a farewell disco for exchange students the Saturday before they go. I'll find out where that is this year and maybe we can wangle our way in!"

"Yeah, *right*!" I grinned. "How do you sneak in past teachers who know who you are?"

"Well, I dunno … maybe we could—"

"Where're *they* going?" Sandie interrupted Kellie's lame-brain argument, as Kyra screeched her chair back and sauntered off, waving at Jen to follow her.

"They're not…"

"They are!"

"They're not…"

"Oh, yes they are!"

"This I've *got* to see!"

Yep, while the rest of us had been *talking* about The Dare, Kyra had silently risen to the bait and headed off without a word to *do* The Dare, obviously dragging Jen along as her witness.

"Hey, aren't those two boys the ones who thought Sandie was cute?" Kellie pointed out, squinting at Kyra sashaying between the crowded tables in the direction of the lads from yesterday, Jen trudging faithfully behind.

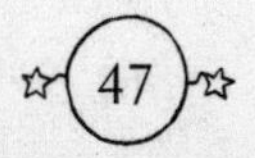

"Don't!" squeaked Sandie, going pink but smiling all the same.

"What's Kyra going to *say* to them?"

Salma might have been the one to speak those words out loud, but it was what we were *all* wondering. And then we watched Kyra; pausing for only a split second beside the lads, but long enough for them to gaze up at her and then laugh.

And no sooner had she got them laughing than she was on her way – with Jen a couple of steps behind – over to the cutlery trays where she stopped and plucked a paper serviette out of the dispenser and gave us a quick wink before she turned and led the way back to our table.

"Nice one, Kyra!" grinned Kellie, high-fiveing our triumphant friend as she slithered herself smugly back into her seat.

"Come on, then!" Chloe demanded. "What did you say?"

"'*Ne le manges pas – ça a un goût de caca!*'" Kyra drawled, looking very pleased with herself.

"One of them had the shepherd's pie," Jen explained, her hand still self-consciously half-covering her mouth.

"And I told him not to eat it 'cause it tasted like poo."

Wow – very witty and clever, I *don't* think. But

witty or not, it meant Kyra had dared to do The Dare.

Gulp.

"Well, that's one down, six of us to go!" Chloe burst out cheerfully.

"*Cuhhhhhh! Cuhhhh!*"

"Are you OK, Ally?" asked Sandie, patting my back as a coughing fit suddenly overtook me.

OK, so maybe sheer panic had made me choke on a slurp of milk there, but was it possible I could pass it off as a bad case of quadruple tuberculosis and stay in bed all week after all...?

THE "WRITE" WAY TO APPROACH LINN

Weird...

Either my bedroom door was squint, or my head was squint. And if you're at all familiar with my head, you'll understand why I thought that second guess was a possibility.

But then I sussed out why it might be the door that was guilty of leaning... Last week, when Billy had popped round to bug me (as he does), we'd ended up playing a game of Tag with Tor, Ivy, Rolf, Winslet and Ben (the dogs were a bit hazy on the rules, but they still had fun). Anyway, Billy was zooming up the attic stairs away from Tor – who was "it" – when he went charging into my room, forgetting to open the door first. When I heard a funny cracking sound, my heart sank, but a quick check of Billy's body parts didn't seem to reveal any broken bones – only a burgeoning bruise or two.

Still, now I could plainly see what had gone "crack"; the hinge at the top of my door was half

hanging out of the splintered wooden door frame.

I'll have to ask Dad to fix that for me, I mused. *Though that'll probably take him for ever, since he never manages to fix anything quickly unless it's bike-shaped...*

OK, you know what I was doing here? Avoiding swotting for tomorrow's maths test. For the last half hour, I'd had my books open in front of me, and managed to pass the time...

a) thinking about my wonky bedroom door,

b) doodling lots of space-age-looking flowers all over the blank page in front of me,

c) wondering if Sandie had told Billy about being flattered by the French boy yesterday (how would Billy take *that* bit of news?),

d) stressing over the fact that Kellie had done The Dare this afternoon, after she'd shouted "*Pardon! Tu as tombé ton tricot!*" at some very grateful exchange student – male, of course – whose jumper had unknotted itself from where he'd tied it round his waist. (Er, that would be two down, five to go, then...)

I couldn't put it off any longer; it had to be done ("Sorry I didn't swot for the test, Mr Horace! There was The Dare and the door and the doodles and stuff, and I just didn't have time!")

Just one problem, I realized, as my hand

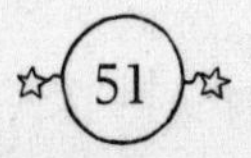

automatically began swirling another space flower – my pen had started to run out. I tried another one (orange – yuk!), but it was pretty much dried up too. I found a pencil that was blunt and kept snapping every time I tried to sharpen it. There was only one thing for it – I'd have to step across the hall and see if the Grouch Queen would deign to lend me a pen from her extensive collection. (I *would* have gone downstairs and borrowed one from Rowan, but it was bound to have a twenty-centimetre-high fuchsia feather attached to it, or something equally as distracting.)

I don't know if it's possible to knock apologetically, but that was the sound I was aiming for when I tap-tapped on Linn's bedroom door. She didn't answer, but I could hear why – she was yapping away on her mobile. She could be on that for hours, and I needed to get my swotting done, so I had to think fast.

Thirty seconds later, I was tentatively sliding open her door, holding a torn sheet of paper out in front of me, like a white flag.

Linn didn't bother stopping her conversation; instead, she shot me a disapproving look and then glanced down at my home-made plea for help. ("Can I borrow a pen, please?", I'd written in blue eye pencil.)

She gave me a barely-there nod, and pointed impatiently towards her bag on the windowseat.

"But I don't see *why*," I heard her say sternly to some unlucky someone-or-other, as I began rummaging in her bag.

You know, that's why notes can be a very useful way to communicate with Linn; they seem to irritate her less and so there's less chance of her shouting at you, I decided, pulling out her immaculate, well-stocked silver vinyl pencil case. (Mine was denim, decorated with ink splodges and empty apart from a few pencil shavings and half a Taz of Tazmania rubber.)

"Look, we've had this planned for *ages*..."

While Linn continued to rant on the phone, I glanced out of the window and saw Rowan down in the back garden, swaying around as she hung up some washing. At first, I assumed that was just my space cadet sister, dancing to the voices in her head or something. Then, with a little glint of evening sunshine settling on something silvery, I realized that she had headphones on – which was why she was happily oblivious to the ferocious cat-fight going on right behind her.

If I hadn't guessed already, the yowling bundle of long-haired black-and-white fur tangled together meant that Fluffy and Tabitha had moved on a step

from claw-slashing to full-on, no-holds-barred wrestling. With teeth. (Just as well Tabitha was owned by Michael the vet – she could get any stitches done for free…)

"…and I just don't think it's fair that you've suddenly decided to invite *her* along, without asking me or Mary or Nadia if we mind."

Uh-oh, I thought, helping myself to a pristine pen and zipping the bag back up. *Is Linn talking about who I think she's talking about?*

"Thanks!" I'd written on the back of my white flag/piece of paper, and I wafted that in Linn's eyeline as I gingerly tiptoed my way out of her room. Linn gave me a little wave in return. On second thoughts, it was more of a case of shooing me out of her room, I think.

"It's just not on, Alfie," I heard her say firmly as I gently pulled her door closed behind me. "You'll just have to see us on Sunday like we arranged, and see *her* another time!"

Urgh … she was moaning on about Rowan, just as I'd sussed.

Y'know, I wished that – like Fluffy – Linn would just chill out, 'cause after all Rowan – like Tabitha – was pretty cute and harmless…

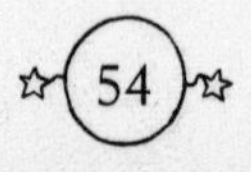

FAVOURS AND FREAK-OUTS

Every Monday morning, I vow that – for the whole week – I won't be tempted by the wicked delights of the school shop. (Quavers and Snickers *might* taste like the food of the gods, but they aren't exactly laden with nutrients, are they?)

Anyway, I *usually* manage to keep my resolution till about, oooh, 11 a.m. on Monday morning when the bell rings for break. But this week I'd done amazingly well – I'd made it all the way to Wednesday morning without crumbling (and only nicked the odd crisp off my friends in the meantime). Anyway, you'd have to be cruel to deny me the pleasure of a packet of Skittles after the trauma of the maths test.

"Y'know, she's *really* winding me up!" Sandie grumbled, as we both shuffled forward in the rugby scrum that masqueraded as a queue in front of the school shop counter.

"Who is?"

Sandie's not much of a grumbler – you could tell

her that her entire wardrobe had spontaneously combusted *and* that a law had been passed that you had to attend school seven days a week, and she'd just come out with "Oh … OK!" – so someone must have *really* got to her.

"Kyra!" she blurted out. "It's just that every time that French lad's around – the one who … *y'know* –"

Little Miss Shy couldn't quite bring herself to say "the one who fancied me". And I wasn't about to blurt it out loud and make her cringe with embarrassment either. Unlike Kyra, it seemed.

"What's she been saying?" I asked, shuffling forward a centimetre in the noisy crush of blazered bods around us.

"You've heard her! It's that stupid 'va-va-va voom!' thing she comes out with." Sandie shook her head wearily, her fine hair flip-flapping in a ponytail as she spoke. "As soon as she sees him, she keeps nudging me hard and saying 'va-va-va blimmin' voom' really loudly!"

"You know what Kyra's like – she's doing it to wind you up," I pointed out, while gently but firmly blocking the way of some horrible Year Seven boys who were trying to wriggle their way to the front of the queue. "She's probably a bit jealous that it's *you* that's got a fan, and not *her*!"

"I wouldn't exactly call him a *fan*," Sandie

mumbled, wriggling her nose after a few seconds of racking her brains. "The thing is, he probably only said –" she paused again, this time to blush – "that compliment thing about me as a joke! I don't think he'd know me again if he tripped over me in the corridor!"

"Uh ... excuse me, please..."

At first, I thought it was just another chancer trying to dodge the queue, only using charm instead of elbows this time. But no; the voice – the hand that was currently tip-tapping on Sandie's shoulder – belonged to ... the va-va-va voom boy. Otherwise known as Sandie's Fan. Or SF, as I suddenly decided to call him, since it was a lot, *lot* quicker to say than va-va-va voom...

Wow.

If SF had liked her big blue eyes from a distance on Monday, then he must have been blown away by them now, in close-up. Specially as Sandie was so gobsmacked that the only response she could make was to open her eyes so wide in surprise that they looked like a pair of sky-coloured satellite dishes fixed to her face.

"There is so many people," SF began hesitantly, gazing straight into Sandie's satellite dishes, "that I ask you, for a favour, to get me some Coke?"

"No problem!" I butted in, grabbing the pound

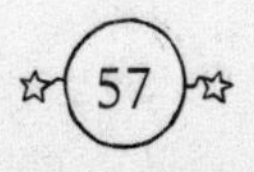

coin from his fingers, since Sandie was incapable of *babbling*, even.

With a smile and a toss of his floppy fringe, SF slid backwards through the crowd, leaving enough distance – and heads blocking his view – for Sandie to risk flashing me an "oo-er!" look of shock.

"Well, I guess he *does* remember you!" I teased her, just as it was our turn to get served.

One minute, one bag of crisps, a packet of Skittles and two Cokes later, we turned and began to push our way out of the throng.

"*You* give it to him!" Sandie whispered, moving her mouth so little she could have easily got an apprenticeship as a ventriloquist.

"No way!" I told her, stepping sideways and avoiding the Coke can and change she was trying to thrust my way.

"*Please*, Ally!"

But it was too late for begging; all of a sudden, the protective layer of people dissolved from around us, leaving nothing but a yawning gap between Sandie and me, and SF and his mate. Sandie may have been gawping directly at him like a bunny in headlights, but I switched my gaze momentarily behind the two lads. Further along the corridor, Kyra and co were hogging a space by a window, waiting for us. And from their craning

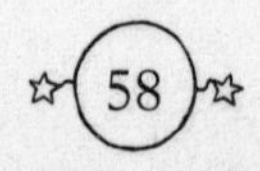

necks and grinning faces, you could tell they were being kept *well* entertained by watching the developing situation with Sandie and you-know-*qui*...

"*Merci,*" smiled SF, stepping forward towards my dumbstruck best buddy. (Smart move on his part – for a moment there I'd half-expected Sandie to turn and run as fast as her size 39s could carry her.)

"*De rien!*" I heard her mumble, shoving the can and the change into his waiting hand, and then zooming off at lightning speed, before he could say another (French or English) word.

"*Go,* Sandie! *Go,* Sandie! *Go,* Sandie!" Kyra whooped, as me and my luminously pink friend hurried towards them.

"*Don't!*" Sandie hissed at Kyra in mortified alarm.

"That was *cool*, Sandie! What did he say to you?!" Kellie whispered, sensing Sandie's desperation for all our friends to act a bit more low-key. It's just a pity Kellie decided to give Sandie a "well done" hug at the same time – SF and his mate were *French,* not *blind,* and if they were looking in Sandie's direction, I'm pretty sure they would have clocked the cringeworthy congratulations that were going on.

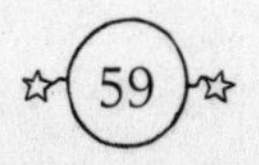

"Never mind what he said to her; it's what she said to him!" I interrupted the back-patting going on.

"What *did* I say to him?" Sandie turned and asked, looking bamboozled.

"You said '*de rien*', which – if I'm not very much mistaken – is French, which – if I'm not also very much mistaken – means—"

"You did The Dare, Sand!" Chloe burst in.

"*Yesss!* Three down, four to go!" Salma laughed, which in turn sent a ripple of dread scurrying down my spinal cord.

As a flurry of squeals and more back-patting and high-fiveing broke out amongst my friends, I dreaded to think what the French lads must have made of us, and was too ashamed to turn round and see. What I *could* scc without turning round was that Jen wasn't really joining in – again. Instead of grinning or giggling or whatever, the best she could manage was a lopsided twitch of the mouth, which I guessed was a (pretty pathetic) attempt at a smile. And then even *that* vanished when she spotted me glancing her way.

"Got to go..." she mumbled, loud enough for only me (who was looking at her) and Kyra (who was standing next to her) to hear.

"What's up with *her*?" Kyra barked, in her usual untactfully loud voice, as Jen attempted to scurry

her way through the throng of yakking exchange students currently hogging every centimetre of floor space in the corridor.

Of course, Kyra blasting off like that inevitably got everyone's attention, and a split second later all our mutual mates had turned their attention from Sandie to Jen's receding figure.

"She's been weird all week…" I replied, keeping my eyes fixed on Jen, who was trying to find a way though the chatting girls and lads in vain, her mutterings of "excuse me" apparently not reaching anyone's ears.

"*EXCUSEZ-MOI!!!*"

Well, *that* unexpected outburst from our usually easygoing friend not only got the attention of the exchange students (who immediately jumped aside and made way for the psycho English girl), but it shook up us lot too.

"Well," shrugged Kyra, checking out the shocked expressions on the faces of the French crew, "I guess Jen *definitely* did The Dare. Look at that lot – they heard her all right, and we did too."

"Along with half of north London," I grumbled, half-joking, half-worried about Jen.

"Is she *that* bugged by having braces?" Salma wondered aloud, her dark eyebrows dipping towards each other in concern.

It couldn't just be that, could it?

No sooner had that thought fluttered into my head, than I had one of those spooky, Mulder and Scully moments: although common sense was telling me that I'd just seen Jen stomp away in the direction of the science block, just to the right of us, I spotted her coming out of the door that led to the girls' loos. And then, blam! I realized that I was looking at her sixteen-year-old sister Rachel. It's really disconcerting whenever you see Rach; she seriously is *so* much Jen's double. Same colour hair, same hairstyle, same round face, same small dark eyes always blinking like the shutter on a camera.

"Hold on a minute; there's Jen's sister – I'm going to have a word…" I told my mates, hurrying away from them before they could say anything, and before Rachel could vanish in the milling crowds.

Rachel was all right for somebody's big sis; she didn't blank you like you were invisible, like you were just a nobody who was her little sister's friend.

"Hi, Ally!" she waved at me, and then made to move away. (Hey, I know I just said she didn't treat you like you were invisible, but she didn't exactly want to be your new best mate or anything.)

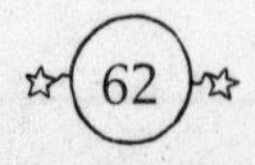

"Rachel – got a minute?"

"Um ... sure!" she nodded, her light-brown bob bobbing just like Jen's. "What's up?"

"Well ... is there something up with Jen? She's been kind of ... *funny* this week."

"Not a big surprise, though, is it?" Rachel shrugged, hugging a couple of folders to her chest. "Not considering what happened at the weekend."

"I *s'pose*..." I shrugged in reply. Maybe I wasn't being very understanding; I'd never had to wear braces, so I'd no idea how bad it might be to have bits of plastic and metal welded into your mouth.

Still...

"I mean, it's been horrible for *all* of us. Not just Jen," Rachel continued. "With the atmosphere at home and everything."

"How come? Just 'cause of her teeth?!" I couldn't help blurting out.

This didn't make any sense – Rachel, and Jen's parents were *all* freaked out about Jen's barely visible brace?

"Her *teeth*?! What are you on about, Ally?" Rachel frowned at me, her black button eyes peering at me as if she was trying to figure out if I was taking the mickey or just plain thick. "I'm talking about our parents splitting up!"

In my head, I wanted to say, "You *what*?", but I

think it came out more like, "Urrgh-*erk*?" Still, Rachel seemed to get the gist.

"She didn't *tell* you?"

I shook my head. Hard.

"Well, our parents told us on Sunday night – that they're divorcing, I mean."

I didn't know what else to do in the totally flabbergasting circumstances, so even though it made no sense I just shook my head again. Maybe I was hoping it would help this insane information sink in…

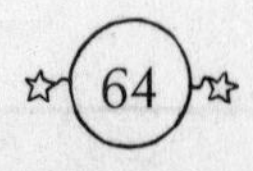

WHITE LIES AND BIG HUGS

So … the two bizarro facts of the matter were:

1) Out of absolutely nowhere, with no hints or clues at all, Jen's mum and dad were getting a divorce.

2) Jen hadn't said a peep about it.

This was all spectacularly weird, and we *had* to find out what was going on.

Excuse me – *I* had to find out what was going on, according to my bunch of mates, who'd volunteered me to track Jen down before break ended and talk to her. What did they take me for? Ricki Lake?

Well, I don't know if Ricki Lake ever gets the collywobbles* when she's about to confront anyone on her show, but my legs definitely got a bad case of the collywobbles when I saw Jen standing outside the closed door of our next class (history), with her head buried in her hands. Gulp.

(*Definition of 'collywobbles': when your body feels like it's made of jelly and you've got custard glooping through your veins instead of blood.)

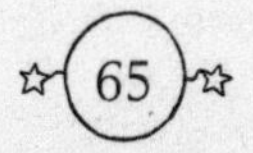

"Jen?" I said, coming up beside her and gently touching her on the elbow.

Oops – I must have accidentally pressed a button and set her off or something; next thing I know, poor Jen's shoulders are shaking so hard it was like an earth tremor had just hit the first-floor corridor of Palace Gates school.

"Ally? What's going on?" a kind voice drifted along the corridor, at the exact same second the end-of-break bell jangled.

I wanted to tell Miss Thomson the truth, seeing as she was my favourite teacher and a really nice person (i.e. human and smiley and patient, unlike other teachers I could mention). But how would that have sounded to Jen, who didn't even know that I knew yet? And blabbing private stuff about Jen's parents in the middle of a hall that had suddenly become rammed with people all scurrying to their various rooms of torture (er, sorry, *classes*) wouldn't do much to help keep the private stuff private.

I didn't have to glance at Jen to know what I should do (I couldn't have anyway, as she'd now burrowed her sobbing face into my chest). There was only one thing *to* do, and that thing was a little white lie.

"Jen hasn't been feeling well all morning," I

fibbed to Miss Thomson. "Can I take her to the nurse?"

Of course, Miss Thomson said "Of course". Yes, I might have been bending the truth, but to anyone looking (and trust me, quite a few people already were), there was no denying that Jen was in a really bad way...

"There you go..."

"*Hic...!* Thanks, Al!" Jen hiccuped, taking the mammoth bundle of toilet roll I'd just torn off the dispenser and passed to her. There was *way* too much; probably enough to mop up Niagara Falls, but when someone's so sobbingly upset as Jen was at that moment, it's very hard not to feel helpless and useless. So, until she decided to tell me what was going on, all I could do was keep her company and pass her the equivalent of a small tree in loo paper.

We weren't in the nurse's office, as you might have guessed. We were sitting (well, Jen was sitting and I was crouching) in the ground-floor girls' loos, third cubicle to the right.

"Izmimummindad!" Jen suddenly blurted out, before burying her head in the paper mountain scrunched up between her white-knuckled fingers.

Because the last twenty minutes or so had been

pretty surreal anyway, at first I couldn't work out what she was on about. "Izmimummindad"? Was that near Trinidad?

And then the penny dropped: I didn't need a Vulcan language decoder, I just had to tune into English spoken with a tear-stained accent. "It's my mum and dad," Jen had said. At last, she was going to start telling me the truth.

"I know about your parents," I told her. Well, told the top of her head, actually.

"You do? *How?!*"

Her face emerged slowly from the damp cocoon of loo paper. With her round face and black button eyes, Jen always reminded me of an old-fashioned doll. But now, with her face pure white and the tears giving her cheeks a waxy glow, she was more like an antique doll than ever.

"I bumped into Rachel…"

OK, that was a teeny white lie too, but Jen didn't need to hear that I'd gone chasing after her big sister to talk about her behind her back.

Jen bit her lip, and looked in danger of shutting up again, so I pushed her for more info. I had nothing to lose, and there was still another small tree's worth of loo roll on the dispenser if my questions upset her too much.

"Why didn't you tell me? Or Kellie or one of the others?"

"Didn't want it to be true," she snuffled. "Thought they might change their minds."

Hmm ... that didn't seem very likely. I mean, you'd hardly blast your daughters with the news that you're divorcing, and then say, "Actually, let's not bother after all!" a couple of days later...

"So, how come your mum and dad are splitting up? I always thought they were really happy!"

That wasn't to say I liked Jen's parents too much – they were the type who pretended to be really arty and laidback, but underneath they were even more strict than some people's very old-fashioned, "you'll-do-as-I-say-young-lady!"-type parents. Growing up, Jen and Rachel might have wanted Barbie dolls and birthday cakes covered with enough icing to make you sick, but instead, they got "educational" wooden toys and home-made carrot cake with no icing. There was a long list of things Jen's mum and dad didn't approve of: watching TV (unless it was documentaries); teen magazines; junk food; dairy products; wheat; to name just a few. I guess that's why Jen loved hanging out in any of our mates' houses – for her there was nothing so deliciously wicked as watching old re-runs of *Buffy the Vampire Slayer* while flicking through a fashion mag and

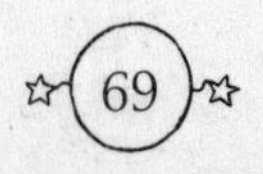

eating as many crisps and cheese sandwiches as she could fit in her mouth in one go.

I mean, when you went round to Jen's, it wasn't like her folks would be horrible to you or anything, but they just had a habit of smiling patronizingly and shooting knowing looks at each other if you happened to mention you'd had a takeaway pizza for your tea the night before, as if your parents were guilty of child cruelty or something. Basically, Jen's parents always seemed like they were in some secret smug club together. But smug or not, Jen still loved them, and to find out they were splitting up must have been like finding yourself in a parallel universe where everything looks the same … but isn't.

"*I* thought they were happy too, till half past seven on Sunday night!" Jen sniffed, balling up a section of snotty tissue and chucking it on the floor.

"So?" I asked, automatically picking up the crumpled snot rag and dumping it in the bin by the loo. (Even in weird situations, I've got this thing about litter.)

"*So* … you know how my dad plays in a folk band a couple of nights a week?"

"Uh, *yeah*…" I said, racking my brain cells and remembering that I *did* know that.

"Well, it turns out he's fallen in love with the ukulele player!"

I was stunned into silence for a second, firstly 'cause I was trying to figure out what a ukulele *was* exactly, and secondly...

"Er ... the uku-wotsit player..." I mumbled.

"Yeah?"

"It is... It *is* a woman, isn't it?"

Now it was Jen's turn to be silent for a second, till – amazingly – she started to snigger through her snottiness.

"Yes, of *course*!" she managed to answer me, a welcome grin splitting her face. "Did you think my dad was running off with a *guy*?!"

"Well, y'know ... he *might* have done! It's a free country! I mean, our neighbours Michael and Harry are boyfriend and girlfriend! Er, boyfriend and *boyfriend*!" I burbled, embarrassed at getting it wrong. "And anyway, I didn't know if there were that many female uku-wotsit players out there!"

Then I realized it didn't matter that I was embarrassed, or that I didn't know what a uku-wotsit was in the first place (it could have been a giant underwater trumpet, for all I knew) – all that mattered was that Jen had got the whole horrible thing off her chest, and that she was smiling for the first time in days.

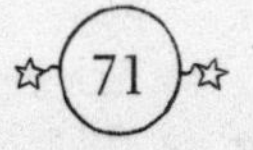

As for me, one thing was for sure – what Jen was going through at home definitely made the huffy hassles between my sisters seem like a storm in a doll-sized teacup by comparison…

WHAT'S ANOTHER WHITE LIE (OR TWO)?

"Poor Jen..." mumbled Sandie.

"Yeah, poor Jen..." Salma nodded.

It was hard to talk about anything but "poor Jen" today. Now, here we all were at the end of the school day, hovering by the main gate and mulling it over again – *without* Jen, who'd gone home "sick" after our confessional in the loo this morning.

"Hope she's all right," said Chloe. "Maybe I'll give her a phone later..."

"But remember what Jen said to Ally," Kyra butted in. "She told her she didn't mind the rest of us knowing; she just didn't want us to make a fuss."

"She doesn't want us to keep asking her about it, *that's* what she said," I reiterated.

I understood that totally; all the years Mum was gone, I didn't particularly want to talk about her too much with my mates – it made me a bit too sad.

"Poor Jen..." Sandie sighed softly, for about the hundredth time.

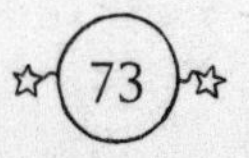

Meanwhile, while the rest of us were "poor Jen"ing, Kellie had a bit of a pout on.

It wasn't that she was exactly sulking or anything. And it wasn't as if she didn't feel bad for our mate (she did). I guess it was because she had some truly *top* news, and it was being overshadowed by what had happened with Jen. Oh, yes, our very own gossip guru had been very hard-working: apparently, Kellie was told by Shantelle Dawson that Gemma Soames overheard Jamila Singh say that *she'd* heard that Ellie Stevens's big brother Gareth – who's in the year above us – knew for a *fact* that some of the pupils looking after some of the exchange students might possibly, *maybe* take them to the KFC up on Crouch End Broadway after school today.

(Phew.)

So I suppose that after going out of her way to gather all this prized information, Kellie couldn't help being just a *little* bit disappointed that her excellent detective work hadn't got everyone as excited as she'd hoped. She'd expected that the whole gang of us would charge up the Broadway for chicken nuggets and spying as soon as the end-of-day bell rang. Instead, we were hovering here, yakking on about Jen's trauma.

"Erm ... why don't we talk about all this while

we're walking to the Broadway?" Kellie suggested, as unsubtly as could be.

"Can't come – Billy's on his way to meet me," said Sandie.

"Me neither – I've got to pick up my brother from his friend's house," I chipped in.

"But, Ally, why can't you get one of your sisters to pick Tor up?" Kellie asked, unwilling to let me go so easily.

"'Cause I already told my mum *I'd* do it."

"But Ally, it would be so much more *fun* if you came!" Kellie whined imploringly.

"Thanks *very* much, Kel! *Sorry* the rest of us are such a disappointment to you!" Chloe huffed, pretending to take offence.

"You *know* what I mean, Chloe," Kellie told her placatingly. "And you too, Sandie – I think it's a shame you can't come. What if that French lad that likes you is there?"

"Yeah, Sandie!" Kyra grinned, suddenly perking up since there was a bit of teasing to be done. "Can you imagine how disappointed the va-va-va voom boy will be if we walk in there and you're not with us?!"

Now this sort of teasing was *exactly* the reason I was delighted to have Tor as an excuse to avoid Kellie's stalking expedition to KFC. Even though

I'd got Jen smiling in the end, I was still feeling a little glumsville after witnessing her misery at first hand today, and the last thing I was in the mood for was being egged on by my so-called mates to do the dumb old Dare.

"Kyra!" squeaked Sandie, spots of indignant pink on her cheeks. "Will you shut up about him? And stop calling him the 'va-va-va voom boy'!"

"Why? He's cute!" Kyra shrugged. "I'd be *well* chuffed if he fancied *me*!"

"Well, *you* can have him!"

"Huh?"

The "huh?" was accompanied by a screech. The screech was the sound of the brakes on Billy's bike as he pulled up beside us out of nowhere. The "huh?" was Billy's response to catching the tail end of a conversation he wasn't too sure he liked.

"It's nothing. It's just Kyra – she's just trying to wind me up," Sandie mumbled, her blue eyes so wide and her whole face so flushed that she might as well have had "GUILTY!!" tattooed on her forehead.

"Yeah? Well, she's a bit of an expert at that, isn't she?" Billy grinned.

But he couldn't fool me. From the way he was fidgeting with the peak of his baseball cap, you could tell he was still a bit confused.

"True ... that's just one of my many talents," Kyra smirked back at him.

Kyra might have been unsubtle, but at least she wasn't landing Sandie in it, when it came to Sandie's Fan. I think – along with the rest of us – she'd just sussed that Sandie hadn't gone out of her way to mention SF to Billy...

"So, who could Kyra have?" asked Billy, turning back to Sandie, his cheerful grin slipping uncertainly.

"Who what-ty?"

I think Sandie was struggling to sound normal, but the squeak in her voice would only have sounded normal if she'd happened to be a fieldmouse who'd just swallowed the contents of a helium balloon.

"You said, 'Well, you can have him,' to Kyra, when I cycled up just now."

OK, so I could feel my third white lie* of the day coming on, but you've got to help a best friend, haven't you? Even, er, if it means lying to your *other* best friend...

(*My first white lie had been telling Miss Thomson that Jen was sick; my second white lie, well, I'll explain about that in a minute.)

"They were arguing about boy bands," I told Billy, scratching a non-existent itch on my nose so

he couldn't spot my telltale mouth twitch. "You know ... which ones were gorgeous and which ones were uggs."

"Oh ... OK!"

Poor Billy, he gazed at me like such a love-struck, trusting, gormless puppy that I wanted to hug him and ruffle his hair.

Boy ... did I feel like a rat for fibbing to him. Sandie should have just told him about SF chucking a compliment her way. Now it felt like it was some deep, dark secret, when, really, it was a whole heap of innocent nothing.

"Hey – check it out!" Chloe suddenly burst out, turning her red-haired head to follow the crowd just passing us; half of them French and interesting, half of them Crouch End-ish and ordinary. Seemed like Kellie's contacts might be right; looked like a gang outing up the Broadway *was* on the cards.

"Va-va-va voom!" smirked Kyra, nudging Sandie in the ribs out of habit, without – eek! – thinking how it might look to Billy.

Then it got worse. SF – slap bang in the middle of the crowd – made a huge, obvious point of smiling and waving at Sandie. And what did Sandie do? Wave and smile back.

You know those RSPCA ads of sad-eyed dogs

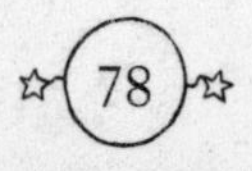

that have been cruelly mistreated by their uncaring owners? That is *exactly* what Billy looked like right now...

OK, so I promised I'd tell you what the second white lie had been.

Well, I'm ashamed to say that I'd fibbed to my friends, and used my little brother as a reason not to hang out with them. It's just that I knew they'd never take no for an answer; "not being in the mood" isn't a viable excuse to bossy types like Chloe and Kyra. Put on the spot like I was after school, the only way out as far as I could see was to invent some babysitting duties or fake a *faint*.

Actually, I half thought Sandie might faint when she sussed the effect of her wave and smile on Billy. As they ambled awkwardly away from us – Sandie with her flushed face pointing to the pavement and Billy with his baseball cap practically pulled down to his nose – I didn't suppose today's after-school date was exactly going to be a glowing, slushy love-fest. I'd have to phone Sandie later and see how they got on. Or maybe I should phone Billy... I tell you, it's kind of tough to know where your loyalties lie when your two best mates are dating.

"Tor, can you ask Rowan where the iron is."

Linn's voice was drifting out of the living room as I walked in the front door and gingerly began stepping over the three sleeping dogs cluttering up the hallway.

"Hi, Ally!" said Tor, trotting out of the living room and heading for the kitchen.

"Hi, Tor," I replied, pausing to scratch Rolf's head as he woke up and nuzzled his wet nose against my ankle.

I was well up for giving Rolf all the extra attention he wanted at the moment; Ben might have settled into our household no problem, but that wet nose of Rolf's was a little out of joint thanks to the way Winslet seemed to have fallen for Ben's undeniable blond good looks. Even now, lost in doggy snooze-land, she had curled her short hairy self right up close to Ben's golden-furred chest. It must be hard when you're a scruffy rescue mutt and your girlfriend falls for the canine equivalent of David Beckham.

"Linn says where's the iron!"

"Well, you can *tell* Linn that I don't know *where* the iron is."

Still scratching Rolf's ear, I watched as Tor trotted out of the kitchen, gave me a quick grin, and disappeared back into the living room.

"Rowan says she doesn't know where the iron is."

"Well, can you tell her that that's very strange, since I saw her taking it up to her room this morning!"

Tor was off again, watched by me, Rolf, and now Winslet, who looked a little grumpy that her afternoon nap was being disturbed by loud voices and Tor's back-and-forth trotting.

"Linn says that's very strange 'cause she saw you or something."

"Well, you tell Linn from me that..."

Hey, this was clever – my sisters were managing to have a row without actually talking to each other!

Fascinating as it was to listen (and watch) this triangular argument, someone had to answer the phone that had suddenly started ringing, and I didn't want yet *another* row breaking out over something so dumb. ("Tor, can you tell Rowan to get that?" "Tor, tell Linn to get it herself!")

"Hello?"

Scurrying over to grab the receiver, I'd missed the rest of Rowan's latest response, mainly 'cause ring tones send Ben into a demented barking frenzy (a little habit of his I'm sure we'll all get used to in time), and Winslet and Rolf had decided to harmonize with an ear-splitting howl or two.

"Uh ... Ally?"

Ker-*floop*.

That was the sound of my heart doing a belly-flop at the unexpected sound of Alfie's voice. It gets me every time – just the sound of him saying my name. (Yes, I *know* I'm sad.)

"Um, hello. Do you want to talk to –"

I paused, about to come out with "Linn" on automatic pilot, since that's who Alfie always asked for – until a few weeks ago, of course, when life got confusing with him and Rowan dating.

"Actually, I, uh ... I wanted to talk to you, Ally, if you've got a minute."

"Me? Why?"

Now it was my turn to sound like a fieldmouse on helium. What on earth would Alfie want to talk to *me* about? But whatever it was, of *course* I had a minute. I had as many million, trillion minutes as Alfie wanted.

"Listen, Ally ... I need your help."

OK, so he *hadn't* confessed that he'd made a terrible mistake and realized now that *I* was the sister he truly loved. So what? Alfie needed my help – *my* help – and that made my heart ker-*floop* all over again...

CHLOE AND THE BIG, SCARY TOE

It's not often that Chloe shuts up for long. And it's not often that you see her porcelain-white skin take on a distinct tinge of pale spinach.

The green glow and the lack of yakking were both down to the hygiene talk our entire year's worth of girls had just been forced to sit through, courtesy of our school nurse, Mrs Owuzu (Mr Mercer from the PE department had the wondrous pleasure of talking to the boys – and dealing with their squirming and embarrassed snickering). Anyway, Mrs Owuzu babbled on about much gruesome germ-related yukky stuff, but I think Chloe finally lost it when Mrs Owuzu showed a slide of a toenail totally eroded with some kind of gungy, fungal horribleness. I can't say I was exactly entranced by the vision of a metre-square enlargement of a cruddy big toe in glorious barf-a-rama, but it didn't get me gagging like poor Chloe.

Mind you, the reason I hadn't found our school

nurse's gory tales too bad was because I'd spent *most* of the lesson ignoring bacterial and fungal infections and daydreaming about something far, far nicer (called Alfie).

"Hey, Chloe – tell them what happened yesterday!" I suddenly heard Kellie urge our green friend, while pointing her finger vaguely in the direction of me, Sandie and Jen.

"*You* tell them," mumbled Chloe, her characteristic bounce still mighty deflated.

"*I'll* tell them," Kyra took over. "She only went and did The Dare!"

"Yeah?"

That was me – raising my eyebrows at the news and hoping I looked suitably impressed. Not that I was. Not now that it meant there were five down and two to go, and the two consisted of me and Salma. (Lucky us...)

"Where? How?" said Sandie, directing her questions at Kyra, Kellie and Salma, since Chloe had suddenly veered off in the direction of the loos, muttering, "Back in a minute," as she went.

Kyra opened her mouth to reply, but Kel and Salma seemed just as keen to spread the news. And so me, Sandie and Jen got the gist of it, barked in overlapping soundbites from all three at once.

"KFC..."

"...and we were sitting right next to a bunch of French boys..."

"...but not SF..."

Oops – the other girls had adopted the nickname I'd given Sandie's Fan and now the very mention of it had given Sandie an instant case of beetroot cheeks, I noticed.

"...no, 'cause he was sitting over by the window..."

Though I don't know *why* Sandie was blushing; after all, she'd phoned me last night and told me that Billy had been surprisingly OK once she'd explained to him about SF and how innocent it all was. She said he'd just shrugged and said, "Fine," and then changed the subject. (Sounded suspiciously grown-up and mature for Billy, I have to say.)

"...and there weren't any spare seats *there*..."

"...but then there were beside these *other* lads..."

Now I sneaked a look at Jen, and was pleased to see that she looked a bit more like herself today, even if she *had* told Kellie in English first period that she didn't want to talk about her parents' divorce and everything right now, same as she'd said to me yesterday morning in the loo.

"...anyway, we'd *only* just sat down when Chloe..."

"...yeah, listen to this – Chloe only leans over and says to one of 'em..."

"...*Puis-je avoir ton ketchup, si tu n'en veux pas?*"

"...which was pretty funny, since she already *had* six sachets on her tray!"

Maybe I hadn't been listening properly or maybe my French was pretty rotten – or a bit of both – but I didn't really understand what it was that Chloe had said (except for the fact that it had something to do with ketchup), and so I didn't get what the joke was, or why exactly Kyra, Kellie and Salma were cracking up.

Mind you, I wasn't the only one.

"Think I'll go and check on Chloe," Sandie said aloud, to anyone who was listening, i.e. only me and Jen, since the other three were still cackling away.

"I'll come with you."

"Me too," I chipped in after Jen spoke – I didn't want to be left behind in case Kyra suddenly took it into her head to forcibly grab some passing exchange student and force me and Salma into talking to the poor boy...

One minute later, and I'd wangled myself a perfect pocket of peace, where I could spend a few minutes running through my conversation with

Alfie, without interruption. OK, so I was in a loo cubicle, if you want to know – Sandie and Jen were over by the sinks, doing such a great job of holding Chloe's hair while she puked that they didn't see me scuttling off. (Good grief, it was like Rolf and the straw all over again.)

And so, ignoring the chatter – and barfing – going on outside, I parked my bum on the lid of the toilet, rested my feet on the back of the cubicle door, closed my eyes so that the latest graffiti on the walls didn't distract me from my daydreaming, and cast my mind back to Alfie's phone call yesterday evening...

"Ally, you're so much more fanciable than Linn and Rowan."

OK, so that's what I thought Alfie said at first – but it was an easy mistake to make, what with Ben, Winslet and Rolf still yelping and yowling about five centimetres away from my eardrums.

"Shut *up*! Oh – not you! The dogs, I meant! Um, what did you say just now?"

Thank goodness video phones weren't everyday household items. All Alfie would have been able to see of me was a scarlet face peeking out of a school shirt, with wild eyes and cold sweat breaking out on my forehead. That and three daft dogs bounding around in the background.

"I said, I need your advice, Ally, 'cause you're a lot more sensible than Linn and Rowan."

Ah, more *sensible*. Not fanciable. Of course. Boring, but true.

"Right. OK. Er ... fine."

Well, perhaps he wouldn't think I was that sensible after all, not unless I pulled myself together and spoke in sentences, like a normal person.

"It's my eighteenth birthday on Sunday ... and I've got plans to go out with Linn and our other mates," he drawled in his lovely, laidback voice. "Thing is, I really want Rowan to come along too, but Linn says she won't come if *Rowan* comes. I don't know why she's being like that. I mean, it's *my* birthday ... I should be able to invite who I want, right?"

Yeah, if you were dealing with a rational person, and not someone like Linn, who is always 1000% sure they're never wrong...

"Right!" I heard myself agree with him, all the same.

Then it dawned on me that I'd witnessed part of that argument for myself, when I'd been in Linn's room a couple of nights ago, borrowing a pen. I was just thinking about this, when I realized that Alfie was silent, obviously waiting for me to say something more useful than just "right".

"Look, I can't exactly *talk*," I whispered into the receiver, worried that either of my sisters could overhear my secret squirrel conversation with Alfie. Though I didn't suppose they really *could*, not over the top of our nutty dogs, *or* over the top of the noise war they now seemed to be waging with each other, i.e. every time the telly went louder, so did the radio in the kitchen. Had Tor got bored of helping them trade insults, I wondered?

"God, yeah … of course, they're both there, right?"

"Right," I repeated.

"OK … um, so call Linn … 'Bart', and Rowan … 'Lisa' or something."

"S'cuse me?"

"So they don't know you're talking about them."

Ah! A coded conversation! *I* could do that…

"OK, I get it. So … have you … um … tried talking to *Bart* about how you, er, feel?"

Ha! That was a truly useless thing to suggest to Alfie, since a) I'd already heard him trying to talk to Linn/Bart about how he felt, and b) I knew from personal experience that it was a pretty dumb idea too. (If you wanted to *live*, that is.)

"Yeah … but Linn just says she doesn't want to hang out with Rowan and that's that. And then Rowan doesn't want to talk about it either – she

just wants to bury her head about the whole thing. You know them both better than anyone, Ally. What d'you think I should do?"

Stop seeing Bart and Lisa and hang out with me instead, I felt like offering, but (d'oh!) didn't.

"Maybe you could write Bart a note," I said instead with a shrug, as if he could see that. "It worked for me the other night. And if you give it to her and then run away, she can't shout at you!"

"That's brilliant – I could write her a *note*! You're a genius!" Alfie exclaimed, as if I'd just come up with the secret of the universe, for goodness' sake. Wow – how cool was it to seem smart in my hero's eyes?

And then I had to go and spoil it (natch).

"But, like, you don't have to write it in blue eyeliner or anything!"

So I was just trying a lame bit of wit, but since Alfie didn't have the faintest idea what I was on about, that all came out about as funny as a toe with a scary fungal infection.

"Ally! You coming?" yelled Sandie, battering on my cubicle door and jarring me out of my daydream as much as the violent trilling of the end-of-break bell.

"Just a sec!" I yelled back, then yanked the flush lever hard so it would look like I'd genuinely

needed to use the loo and hadn't just skived off and left Sandie and Jen to deal with Chloe's puke-a-thon.

You know, why hadn't the bell come just a split second earlier, so my daydream could have ended at the part when Alfie was calling me a genius, instead of ending at the bit where I sounded like the dumbo that I am…?

TEETH, CLAWS AND EVERYTHING

It was *totally déjà vu*.

Like some kind of spooky photocopy of yesterday afternoon, Kellie had put on her detective hat and found out where the French kids were maybe, *possibly* hanging out after school; my mates were planning on yet more stalking; and I had used the exact same excuse to get out of it.

"You've got to pick Tor up *again*?" Kelly had quizzed me.

"Uh-huh!" I'd nodded, wondering when I'd got into this bad habit of letting little white lies trip off my tongue so easily. And wondering *when* exactly little white lies could be described as proper, full-blown lies.

But whatever … after some useless attempts at persuasion from Kellie and co, I got out of the stalking session and headed for home. Jen had done the same, but unlike me, no one had tried to persuade her to change her mind, not in the circumstances.

The only difference from yesterday was that Sandie had given in. "Well, Billy knows this is all just a laugh!" she'd told me, before our other mates dragged her off in the direction of the skating rink at Alexandra Palace.

Oh, yeah?

I might have believed that if Billy hadn't told me the exact opposite twenty minutes later...

"So this 'voo-voo' guy—"

"Va-va-va voom," I gently set Billy straight, though it didn't exactly matter. "That's Kyra's nickname for him."

"Whatever. What's *really* going on with him and Sandie, Ally? Tell me the truth!"

Poor Billy – he was in a right state. For a start, he hadn't touched any of the crisps or biscuits Mum had brought out on a tray for us (v. unusual for the human dustbin, let me tell you). *And* he must have cycled over from Muswell Hill at the speed of light (probably flattening a few dogs and their owners in the park on the way), 'cause his white school shirt was so wet with sweat that you'd think he'd taken a short-cut via the boating lake, and started a trend for underwater cycling while he was at it.

"Sorry to interrupt." Mum smiled, tiptoeing

barefoot across the grass to us. "But let's get *this* aired too."

Billy had been kind of in awe of my mum since she turned up out of the blue a few weeks ago. I think, for Billy, the idea of having a mum who vanished one day and didn't turn up till four years later was so like something out of *The X-Files* that it freaked him out. Anyway, 'cause he was in awe of her, he just let her whip his obviously damp baseball cap off his head without a whimper. If *I'd* tried to get that away from him, he'd have wrestled me to the ground and been tickling me for dear life by now.

Mum, meanwhile – unaware that Billy looked on her as some beautiful, hippy alien – wandered away from us and pinned the cap on the washing line, next to the school shirt she'd already managed to prise off his back.

"Thank you, Mrs Love," Billy mumbled in her direction, before turning back to me, his arms folded across his bare chest and shivering, even though the garden was baking in the sudden blast of Indian summer sunshine we were having this afternoon. "*So...?*"

"So?" I repeated, playing for time.

I'd been momentarily distracted from what we'd been talking about by the fact that I was having

a separated-at-birth moment. It was just that Billy – with his ridiculous, sticky-up, damp hat hair – suddenly looked *identical* to hairy-headed scruff-bucket Rolf, who was sitting panting happily over by the rabbit hutch, where Ivy and Tor were trying to communicate with Cilla purely by wrinkling their noses and baring their front teeth.

Wow … so Billy and Rolf *didn't* just share a love of junk food, scratching and drooling. Who cared if one of them was a dog, and the other was a human (allegedly). It was like they were cosmic twins…

"Ally?"

"Yeah?"

"I said, is he really coming on to her?"

"SF? I mean, the French boy? No! Honestly!" I tried to convince him, holding out a bowl of nachos before Winslet nabbed them (I could see her out of the corner of my eye, inching across the grass on her tummy, commando-style, with her radar eyes locked on "nibbles").

"Look, I know you're just trying to protect Sandie, 'cause she's your best mate and everything…"

"I'm not!" I squeaked indignantly. "And you're my best friend too!"

"So?"

"So…?"

We'd been here before. We could be here all

night, the tortured mood Billy was in. I'd *still* be here at sunrise tomorrow, with me trying to convince him that Sandie wasn't about to run off and elope with a guy called "Voo-voo" to a small town in Normandy.

"Look, Billy, we heard the guy tell his mate – in French – that he thought she had nice eyes. Apart from that, he asked her to buy him a Coke and he gave her the money. And he waved hello at her yesterday. And that's *all*."

Of course I didn't know what was going on right *now*, up at the skating rink, with Kyra and Chloe and co all egging Sandie on…

"It's just … it's just that she made me feel dumb for being jealous, Ally!"

OK, I was slightly distracted again, but only because Ivy had wandered away from Tor and Cilla and was now happily humming and trickling handfuls of grass on to Billy's bare shoulders.

"Leave Billy and Ally alone, Ivy – they're having a chat," I heard Mum tactfully call over.

"But I'm playing with Billy!" Ivy protested, even though she did as she was told and padded off towards Mum's motioning hand.

"Why?" I said to Billy, forgetting for a second what I was saying "why" to, but hoping it was the right question to ask till I could remember.

"'Cause she kept giggling when she was telling me, like it was some silly joke, and I was being silly too if I didn't see it that way!"

"Did you tell her that?" I quizzed him.

"Well, *no*..."

Communication: sounds fancy, but all it means is talking to people, listening to their points of view and letting them hear yours. Sounds easy, huh? Pity no one I knew seemed able to do it. Not my best friends, not my sisters and – by the looks of it – not even my cat...

"Fluffy, *noooooo*!" I suddenly found myself shouting, for the second time that week.

It's funny how quite shocking events happen in what feels like slow motion *and* all speeded up at the same time. The way Billy bounded upright; *that* felt like it was in slow motion, but the cat-fight itself – it was just one hyper-speed blur of fur, claws and everything *hurtling* around the lawn in a ball of black-and-white fluffiness.

All the sounds in the garden merged together too: me shouting, Tor yelling, dogs barking, Fluffy and Tabitha yowling, Ivy crying, and Billy yelping – but only once he'd torn the two cats from each other, and then torn Fluffy's claws out of his bare chest. (Ouch.)

What a hero.

I tell you, if Tor and Ivy hadn't got there first, I'd have been hugging Billy too.

"Why's Fluffy fighting Tabitha all the time?" Tor sniffled, his head leaning against Billy's (scratched) chest, and his eyes following elderly Tabitha as she bounded up and over the wall to safety.

"Like I said before, it's just a territory thing," said Mum, kneeling in front of Tor, Billy and Ivy, while holding on tight to Fluffy, just in case she fancied chasing after Tabitha or attacking Billy's chest again.

"Huh?" Tor sniffled some more.

Thankfully, Ivy didn't seem so distressed any more – she was still hugging one arm around Billy's leg, but with the other she was jamming her pink teddy bear's head into Billy's school trouser pocket, to see what was there.

"Well, the boy cats don't mind Tabitha," Mum began to explain for Tor's benefit, "but Fluffy and Tabitha are both girls, so I think Fluffy sees Tabitha as a bit of a threat, stealing away Colin and the others."

You know, I'd *already* thought that the situation with those two feuding furballs reminded me of the hassles going on between Linn and Rowan: now it did times *ten*.

"Don't worry – Fluffy and Tabitha will work it

out," I tried to say cheerfully, as I dug in my pocket and handed Billy a crumpled tissue to dab on his scratchy, bleedy bits.

"Yes, Ally's right," Mum nodded, slowly managing to calm Fluffy by scratching her under the chin. "The thing is, Tor, you have to accept that with a territory feud like this, it could take months till it settles down..."

Help! Mum might've been doing a great job of reassuring Tor, but all I could think of was Fluffy and Tabitha = Linn and Rowan. Was it going to take months for the two of them to sort out *their* territory (i.e. Alfie)? I didn't think I could stand it, not *months* of huffs and ignoring each other and talking through Tor. I'd have to take my duvet and a toothbrush and move out to the shed to avoid the stress of it all.

"Um..."

Billy's dumb "um..." dragged me away from my dread of a feud-filled future and into the cat-scratching present. Poor Billy; he looked like he'd been in a bare-chested battle with a barbed-wire fence – and *lost*.

"Um ... Mrs Love – have you maybe got some plasters, d'you think...?"

HONESTY IS THE BEST POLICY. *HONEST*.

Peace...

Billy the hero had left for home, taking his troubles and scratches with him. (Mum had patched him up pretty good – I only noticed one tiny speck of blood seeping through his white shirt when he cycled off.) And for the moment at least, no cats were tearing chunks out of each other, so I could relax and concentrate on stuff like agony aunts in magazines ... they're brilliant, aren't they?

If you're wondering what got me thinking about that, it was 'cause I was lying on the bit of the sofa not already taken up by Rolf, browsing the problem page of one of Rowan's magazines. It was impressive; whatever anyone's problems were, the agony aunt had a sensible, sensitive solution. From exam stress to zit stress, from bad boyfriends to slow-to-grow boobs, this woman had all the answers. (And no, the slow-to-grow boobs letter wasn't from me. Although it could have been.)

Y'know, I sometimes feel like an agony aunt. It's

always *me* that my friends turn to when they want advice. This is all very flattering, but it's a very tiring and poorly paid job. I mean, the agony aunt who did this magazine column, she got a proper wage for her trouble – all I got was my ear bent.

It's exhausting too, when you're using valuable brain power to figure out what to do about other people's hassles. Specially when a girl needs all the brain power she's got to do stuff like her homework. You know something? *That's* why I was lying on the sofa, reading a magazine instead of studying: Billy and Alfie and Rowan and Jen, in their own ways, they'd sucked my mind dry over the last few days. (Funnily enough, Jen had probably moaned to me the *least*, even though she had *much* more reason to moan than the others.) But whatever … I'd have to give my frazzled brain cells time to recharge, wouldn't I? Oh, yes, lying about and reading magazines was medicinal. It wasn't skiving at *all*…

(Who was *I* kidding.)

"Look, Ally, *look*!"

It wasn't totally peaceful lying on the sofa, though, not with Dolly Parton warbling about growing up as an itty-bitty hillbilly at full volume, *or* with the line-dancing masterclass that was going on in the living room.

I lifted the magazine and peered in the direction of Ivy's voice.

"Very nice!" I lied through my teeth, as Mum taught some corny, swivelly, hand-clapping dance steps to Ivy and Tor, who were both in their jim-jams.

This child cruelty was all Dad's fault – for something (naff) to do when Mum wasn't around, he'd started going to line-dancing classes. Now that she'd come back for good, Dad was getting his own back on Mum (it seemed to me) by forcing her to come with him. Amazingly, Mum apparently enjoyed last night's class, and was now inflicting what she'd learnt on her two youngest children. Possibly because she guessed that me, Rowan and Linn might threaten to leave home if she tried to get any of us to join in.

"Ally – dance!" Ivy demanded, stomping her feet in time in her all-in-one pink bunny suit.

To one side of Ivy, Mum's long hippy cotton skirt swished and swung against her legs, and on the other, Tor – dressed in his favourite PJs – was frowning hard in concentration, which was pretty funny, really. I mean, it's not *every* day you see Spiderman taking line-dancing lessons.

"I can't, Ivy – my legs have run out of batteries," I fibbed, earning a knowing grin from my mum. "I'll just watch!"

With that, I began moving my magazine slowly back down in front of my eyes, and hoped Ivy wouldn't notice.

It would have been a lot easier to read my magazine/avoid doing my homework in my room, but Dad was trying to fix my door right now and making such a crash-bang-walloping noise about it that you'd think he was building an *ark* up in the attic, instead of trying to repair one dodgy little hinge. (Like I said before, DIY doesn't exactly come naturally to him.) Between country music warblings and the racket upstairs, I'd decided the living room was marginally less noisy. And that's not saying much.

"*...and don't forget, honesty is the best policy,*" I began to read, roughly where I'd stopped. "*Sometimes you've got to be tough on people and tell them things they don't want to hear. It's for their own benefit in the long run.*"

But hold on a sec ... now I looked at it again, I realized this *wasn't* the bit I'd been reading when Ivy had dragged my attention away from the problem page. I had no idea what this particular reader's worry was, but that snippet of advice from

the agony aunt ... somehow it made a small light-bulb go ping! in the dark recesses of my mind.

"Sometimes you've got to be tough on people and tell them things they don't want to hear. It's for their own benefit in the long run."

Hmm ... it was something to do with telling people things they didn't want to hear. Maybe that's what I needed to do with my friends and family. Maybe I had to get tough too and slap some hard-hitting honesty their way. Me, Ally Love – amateur agony aunt!

All fired up now, I began to stack up a "To Do" list in my mind:

• Tell Linn that Alfie's fed up with her attitude. (Preferably do this while wearing full body armour.)

• Tell Linn she's upsetting Rowan.

• Tell Rowan to stop being a wimp and stand up for herself where Linn's concerned.

• Tell Sandie to be more sensitive to Billy's trodden-on feelings.

• Tell Billy to tell Sandie he's upset, instead of pretending he's OK to her and then coming whinging to me.

This was good. I could make a difference. But, er, maybe before I started sorting out everyone *else's* problems, I should sort one of my very own,

by being totally and utterly honest about how I was feeling…

"Oh! Thought you were joining in with us there!" Mum laughed, as I bounded up off the sofa, waking Rolf while I was at it.

"Got to make a phone call," I told her, hurrying out into the hall, and closing the living-room door behind me to drown out Dolly Parton's "yee-hah!"s.

Grabbing the phone off the hall table, I settled myself on a step on the staircase, took a deep breath and got started.

"Hi, Mrs Brennan – it's Ally."

"Oh, hello, Ally, love – I'll just give her a call."

Quickly, I held the phone away from me – Mrs Brennan's lungs were mighty powerful when she was calling for one of her kids. I think she must have been an opera singer or a foghorn in a past life.

"Chloooooo*EEEEEEE*!! It's All*EEEEEEEEEEEE*!! For *YOOOOOO*!!"

With that yell out of the way, I stuck the receiver back to my ear and waited.

Yep, I was going to start this honesty-is-the-best-policy business with Chloe. If I could get this one thing off my chest, then I'd feel brave enough to go and do everything else on my list. Hey, maybe by the end of the night my sisters' feud would be over

and Sandie and Billy would be all loved-up and happy again!

"Yep? What's up?"

"Just thought I'd phone and say hi," I began, feeling my heart pitter-patter.

"Well, hi. But look, my cousins are visiting so I can't talk for long."

"That's OK – I just wanted to say something quickly."

Chloe didn't say anything in reply, but I could sense a silent question mark waft down the line from her phone to mine.

"It's just about The Dare."

"Yeah?" Chloe said, suddenly sounding interested. "Have you *done* it?"

Ugh. I *wish*...

"No – that's what I'm phoning for. To tell you I don't want to *do* The Dare."

"Ha! Nice try, Al – but you don't get out of it *that* easy!"

"No, but I *really* don't want to do it, Chloe!"

"Ha, ha, ha, ha! Very funny!"

"Honestly, Chloe – my head goes twisty every time I think about doing it. I'd be so embarrassed to—"

"Yeah, yeah, *right*! Anyway, got to go, Ally – my cousin's calling me."

"But—"

"See you tomorrow!"

Well, *that* went spectacularly well. *Not*.

So much for being honest and getting things off my chest. Before, I felt stressed out by The Dare. Now, I felt stressed out by The Dare AND pretty hopeless for not being able to get my point across to Chloe without her laughing in my face (well, not strictly speaking in my face, but you know what I mean).

But there was the problem page, sitting next to me on the stairs, with the "honesty is the best policy" letter staring up at me, daring me to have another go, to make a difference, and not to be put off just because Chloe had her cousins round and was more interested in hanging out with them than listening to what I was wittering on about in my useless way.

Linn's in her room – you could go upstairs right now and tell her what she needs to hear! said the amateur agony aunt in my head, trying to stir a little confidence back into my original plan.

Er, or you could leave that till another time and maybe just do something else right now, like give Jen a call first, just to say hi ... said the complete coward part of me.

Yeah, but Jen wanted a bit of space, remember,

the amateur agony aunt pointed out.

Yeah, but then again, I'm just giving her the chance to talk, in case she's changed her mind, answered the cowardly part of me, which was – let's face it – using Jen as an excuse not to confront Linn.

Guess which voice I listened to?

"Oh! Um ... hi, Mrs Hudson."

Wow – how awkward. When I was inputting Jen's number just there, I was so busy chucking my "To Do" list in a waste-paper bin in the corner of my mind that I hadn't thought about the fact that it was perfectly possible for one of Jen's parents to answer the phone.

Now what was I supposed to say? Something like, "So! I hear you're getting divorced! *That's* nice!"?

"Hello, Ally," Mrs Hudson replied, as I panicked. "Sorry, but Jen's not in right now – she went round to Chloe's for tea."

"Oh. Oh, OK. That's great. Thank you. *Bye!*"

I don't think I've ever been so glad to get off the phone. Well, apart from the time I phoned for a pizza and found I'd called the local police station by accident. (And no, the sergeant at the Crime Desk *didn't* laugh when I asked for a pepperoni pizza with extra cheese, please.)

It was only when I put the phone down that I realized two things: a) Fluffy had curled herself asleep in my lap without me even noticing; and b) Chloe hadn't said anything about Jen being round at hers when I spoke to her a minute ago.

Fluffy acting like a cute cat instead of a ninja warrior? Jen supposed to be somewhere she wasn't?

As Alice in Wonderland once said, curiouser and curiouser…

SALMA AND THE ACCIDENTAL SPLAT

I was doomed.

That's what I lay awake in bed and thought all last night, staring up through the skylight at the full moon staring back down at me.

I was doomed to do Chloe's stupid Dare, and she and the rest of my friends would never let me off with it. And it was all because I was a wuss and couldn't stick to my honesty-is-the-best-policy principles. Well, not enough so that Chloe took me seriously, that's for sure.

Good grief, I'd decided, as I spent a lovely, stress-filled night tossing and turning. I might as well just go up to some poor French guy at school and say, "Hi. I *have* to talk to you because of this dumb dare thing my friends roped me into. I don't know what to say, and I know I sound like an idiot. Please don't hate me. In fact, please shoot me now and put me out of my misery."

The only problem was, my head was too twisty with stress and sleeplessness for me to figure out

how to say all that in French.

See what I mean about doomed?

"Don't say that, Ally!" said Sandie, looking mildly panic-stricken.

Sandie doesn't like the word "doomed"; she says it's "gloomy". *Duh* ... I think it's *supposed* to sound that way. Still, I guess I understand what it's like to have words you hate; with me, it's words like "maths" and "test" when they're run together, or "The" and "Dare"...

"Well, it's all right for *you,*" I told Sandie, as we walked to school together after bumping into each other on the way like we did most mornings. "You've got The Dare out of the way!"

"Yeah, but it wasn't as scary as I *thought* it would be. It was pretty easy, honest!"

I knew Sandie was on my side and was just trying to gee me up, but I couldn't help getting a little grouchy at her. Mainly 'cause she had this sweet smile on her face, like she'd already forgotten a) the manic panic she was in at the school shop the other day when SF asked her to get him a drink, and b) the fact that Billy had been badly put out by the whole SF thing.

"Did you call Billy after I phoned you last night?" I quizzed her, as we both scanned the traffic before crossing the road.

At least that honesty-is-the-best-policy thing had worked on *someone*... After I'd tried (and failed) to get hold of Jen yesterday evening, I'd decided to give Sandie a ring and let her know how Billy was feeling about her, French boys and any potential flirting that was/wasn't going on between them. It was safe to say that Sandie had been stunned when I'd passed on what he'd said – according to her, Billy had pulled off such a good act at not being bothered that he could have waltzed into any drama school without an audition.

"Yes – it was brilliant! We talked for *ages*, and *he* said sorry for getting bugged over nothing and *I* said sorry for not telling him about SF earlier," she explained, once we'd managed to make it to the opposite pavement without being splatted by the bus that had just dropped off millions of uniformed Palace Gates inmates.

"So you're both all happy and loved-up again?" I teased her.

"Oh, yes! And I said, 'Look, baby bear – I mean, *Billy*, we should always tell each other everything.' And he said *definitely*."

"That's good. So he didn't mind that you were hanging out with the others and stalking French boys up at the ice rink after school yesterday?"

Sandie had told me last night on the phone that

– watching (freezing) from the sidelines – she'd got another wave "hello" from SF, as he and his mates sped by in a giant, skating conga line. Or he *might* have been waving her over to join in, Sandie hadn't been sure.

"Er ... I didn't tell Billy about hanging out at the rink," Sandie blinked guiltily at me. "I thought it might bug him again, just when we'd got things sorted out!"

Oh, good *grief*...

"Hi, Sandie! Hi, Ally!"

That was Salma, wandering through the school gate this Friday morning with Chloe, both with their cheeks bulging, matching lollipop sticks poking out of each of their mouths.

For me, it was sort of hard to give her an enthusiastic "hi" in return, when I knew that Salma knew that *I* knew that it was only me and her left in this stupid race that Chloe had started.

Speak of the devil...

"Only today left to do The Dare!" Chloe grinned at me, swivelling her ball-shaped lollipop from one cheek to the other.

Yeah, like I didn't know.

"But then again, we might have *more* time," Salma pointed out, pulling the lollipop out of her mouth and wafting it in the air as she spoke.

"That's if Kellie finds out where any of the French crew are going to be hanging out over the weekend."

Great – talk about extending the agony.

You know that insane plan of mine from earlier in the week? The one about feigning a preferably life-threatening illness? Well, it suddenly seemed like total genius. I didn't think I could take another day's worth of The Dare looming over me, never mind it dragging on for the whole weekend. Maybe I should go to the library at break and see if I could find a medical book so I could look up symptoms to copy?

"I was telling my cousin Ria about the French lads and she said at her school they're doing a German exchange next year and..."

Just as Chloe began filling us all in about some chit-chat with her cousins, I remembered I had something to check up on.

"Hey," I interrupted her, just as the bell rang and the four of us began automatically speeding up towards the main entrance, along with everyone else. "Last night – was Jen round yours for tea?"

"Nope," said Chloe.

That's as far as she got. A whole bunch of over-eager Year Sevens suddenly hurtled themselves bodily towards the entrance, separating me and Salma from Chloe and Sandie momentarily. (Wow

– *those* Year Sevens were keen. It would soon wear off of course.)

Understandably, Salma pulled a face as we found ourselves jostled up the couple of front stairs, and then some thought or other got her smiling again.

"Well, just you and me, then, Al! May the best girl win!"

She had one shoulder on the heavy wooden door, lollipop held up high out of harm's way, and was offering her other hand out to me for a joky, sporting shake. I wasn't exactly in the mood for any "Ha, ha – isn't this whole Dare thing a hoot?!" but I'd have looked a real grouch if I'd ignored her. And so I stretched my own hand out towards hers … but they didn't get a chance to touch, 'cause next thing I knew Salma had disappeared sideways. I mean, one minute she was there, and the next minute … *blam*! And spookily, at the very same time, there was a dull thud and a loud groan from the other side of the door.

Somehow, I managed to elbow out of the way all the gawpers trying to peer over my shoulder and reach over to give Salma a hand up. But she was already in a crouching position, madly brushing away a tangle of long, dark hair from her face and saying "*Pardon! Oh, pardon*!" to someone just out of sight. It was very weird to see glamorous Salma,

normally the coolest of my friends, suddenly lose her cool *big*-style.

"What's up?" I asked, stepping closer to the door and peering around it.

"I think I hit him with the door, Ally!" said Salma in a panic, spinning her head towards me, away from the stunned-looking French boy sprawled on the floor, rubbing his nose.

"OK, well, if you move over a bit I can get inside and go and get Mrs Owuzu," I suggested, spotting that it wasn't just Salma that was blocking the way – the French lad's rucksack had jammed behind the door.

"Don't worry!" Salma yelled at the poor boy, as if his hearing might have been damaged when the door battered against his unsuspecting nose. "My friend – *mon amie* – she's going to get the school nurse and – Oh! Oh, I didn't mean to do that! *Pardon!*"

Nice one.

In an attempt to reach out to inspect the damage, Salma had just whacked her victim on the nose with her lollipop. I decided I'd better hurry and get Mrs Owuzu, before Salma inflicted any *more* damage. As it was, the boy was going to end up going home to the small town of Whatever-it's-called looking like he'd been in a boxing ring, instead of on a school exchange trip to Crouch End.

As I ran down the corridor in search of help – like a good Girl Scout – my heart began to slither downwards, sinking fast to floor level. Urgh … without consciously trying (and injuring someone in the process), Salma had just done The Dare, which meant I was witness to her success and my own fat old failure.

There was only me left to do the stupid Dare, with all my friends' beady eyes on me for the foreseeable future.

Yep, I was *doomed*…

HIDING AND SEEKING

I was doing a very good impression of looking like a swot, sitting at a computer in the school library, five minutes after the end-of-day bell had gone this Friday afternoon.

But staring at that computer screen, I wasn't being a swot, I was actually doing two things: 1) wondering what was up with Jen, and 2) hiding.

Jen … well, Jen hadn't shown up for school today. Was she ill? Had there been more hassles at home? And what was all that stuff about supposedly going to Chloe's last night and then not showing up? I didn't know if phoning Jen was a good idea or not (how awkward would it be if some major family drama was going on?) but maybe I should give it a try, when I got home.

As for the hiding business, well…

"Boo!"

I jumped like mad, thinking at first that it was Mrs Wilkie, the librarian, who had caught me wasting valuable time doing nothing in particular.

"*Don't*, Kyra! You really scared me!" I told her, although I was pretty relieved that it was just her and not Mrs Wilkie breathing down my neck. (But you know, when I thought about it sensibly, there was fat chance of prim, middle-aged Mrs Wilkie coming out with something fun like "Boo!" really. About as much chance of her wearing a pair of deely-boppers and a joke moustache while she was stamping your books out, I reckon.)

"Who did you think it was, Ally?" Kyra laughed scornfully. "An axe murderer?! *'He prowled the young-adult-fiction aisle, on the lookout for his next victim…'.*"

"Yeah, yeah – *very* funny," I droned, hoping I sounded suitably sarcastic.

"Yes, it was. Anyway, what are you doing?" said Kyra, nudging me over and perching her skinny bottom on the threadbare office chair I was sitting on. "Why have you typed those three words on that document?"

"Um … I was just fooling around with the spell-check," I shrugged lamely. "I keyed in 'Jen', 'Kellie' and 'Salma', but the computer didn't recognize them and suggested 'Jet', 'Cello' and 'Salami' instead."

Hey, it seemed like a good idea at the time.

"Why would you want to do that?"

You know, sometimes Kyra has a way of saying stuff that makes you feel *that* big…

"Er … fun?"

"Fun?! Good grief, if you think that's fun, Ally, you must be *really* bored."

OK, so it wasn't what you'd call top-flight entertainment, but I'd figured that if I hung out here in the library for ten minutes or so after the end-of-day bell went, then my friends would give up on me and wander off home or go boy-stalking without me or whatever, and I'd be off the hook. That was my plan (yes, another one). But somehow Kyra had tracked me down.

"Where's everyone else?" I asked, knowing she'd understand who I meant.

"Gone to the bottom field at Ally Pally – Kellie heard there was going to be a five-a-side footie game with some of the exchange students."

"Good," I replied, sounding a bit too obviously pleased.

"So … why are you hiding out here?"

"I'm not hiding out!" I lied, sounding indignant, even though I didn't have a right to be. "I'm fine, I just…"

"You just what?" Kyra asked me, as she leant over and grabbed the mouse, selecting and enlarging my three silly spell-check words – and then deleting them with a flick and a click of a button.

"I just..."

Suddenly I felt deflated; exhausted after a week of stressing over this daft Dare. I know that sounded ridiculous, when you compared it to the sort of emotional week Jen had been through, but stress can come in all shapes and sizes, I guess.

"I just don't *want* to do The Dare," I blurted out. "I can't stand the idea of you and Chloe and everyone watching my every move, waiting for me to go and *launch* myself at some lad."

"Aww ... is Ally-Pally feeling a little bit shy, then?"

"Yes, I am!" I admitted, ignoring Kyra's sarky comment. "Anyway, what's the point of me doing it now? *I* lost – *I'm* the hairy maggot or whatever Chloe said. Can't that just be it *over* with?"

"Nope," said Kyra matter-of-factly, gazing intently at the screen and tip-tapping on the keyboard as I poured my heart out to her. "That wouldn't be fair – *we've* all had to do it. So *you* do too."

"But, Kyra, I just *can't* walk up to some boy and—"

"Don't worry. I'm going to help you."

"How?" I stared at her dubiously.

Side on, with her smattering of dark brown

freckles over her light brown skin and her hair pulled back into a curly topknot, she looked totally sweet and pretty as she continued to gaze at what she was doing on screen. But *I* knew that underneath that sweet, pretty exterior lay a heart of pure *cunning*.

"You know how the Highgate Woods lot hang out at the Town Hall Square after school?"

"Uh … yeah," I said warily.

Course I knew. Everyone at my school knew that. Kids from Highgate Woods school hung out there every afternoon, to chat, flirt, skateboard and look cool. And the reason they looked cool was 'cause they were lucky enough not to have to wear school uniform. Nobody from our school ever tried to hang out in the square with the Highgate Woods lot, mainly because it was their patch, but also because we'd look like real loser dweebs in our blazers and ties amongst a sea of baggy skater jeans and hip band T-shirts.

"Well, *I* heard that some of the French boys are mad on skateboarding, and they're going to go to the square to check out what's going on there. Like this afternoon. Like *now*."

"And you think…?"

"And I think we should go too. It'll be brilliant, Ally – a really good chance to do The Dare. Just

you and me, so you don't have to feel shy; it's not like the others will all be watching you or anything."

"No, but half of Highgate Woods School will," I mumbled, my tummy swivelling at the very thought of trying to mix casually with French lads and cool skateboarders. It felt like being thrown to the lions. Only I guess Crouch End Town Hall Square doesn't look too much like the Coliseum; not with all the pigeons and tramps who hang out there too.

"Don't be so wet, Ally!" Kyra told me brightly, suddenly standing up and obviously expecting me to follow.

Well, it looked like I didn't have much choice in the matter.

Grudgingly, I was just about to pick up my bag and shuffle after her, when I spotted what she'd typed on the screen, in 72pt bold letters, with a drop shadow...

"*Kyra!!*" I hissed at her, madly grabbing at the mouse so I could select and delete the giant swear word before anyone else saw it and we both got detention for the rest of our natural lives.

Kyra gave me a wicked grin in reply, before she turned and swanned off.

What did I tell you about her having a heart of pure cunning?

* * *

"Wonder why Jen's off today... Do you think she's all right? I mean, I *know* she *can't* be all right, with all the upset and everything, but it's hard to know what to do, since she said she didn't really want to talk about it. What d'you think?"

I was babbling on, I knew, and it wasn't just because I was worried about Jen (and I was); it was also because adrenalin was ping-ponging around my body as we walked ever closer to the Broadway, and ever closer to the Town Hall Square just off it. Yikes.

"Jen'll be all right," said Kyra, marching her long legs speedily along the road so that I had to struggle to keep up with her. "She just needs to have some fun, that's all. Just as well there's plenty of *that* happening this weekend!"

"Oh?"

I had done a truly excellent job of cheerfully avoiding my friends most of the day – the morning break had been taken up with much discussion of Salma's nose-splatting exploits (no bones broken in that poor lad's face as it thankfully turned out), and I pretended that our history teacher, Miss Thomson, had asked me to run an errand for her, and so skilfully avoided everyone during afternoon break. So what exactly they had planned for the next two days, I dreaded to think...

"Well, *first* up, Kellie found out that loads of the French crew are going to Park Road Pool tomorrow morning, so we're all meeting there at 10 a.m.," Kyra informed me. "And then at night, Kellie found out that the French department are holding their farewell party in the cricket pavilion at Alexandra Palace, so we're going to meet up and try and wangle our way into that too. Wonder what I'll wear...?"

"Hey, you know – I just thought of something!" I burst out, as we paused beside the Clocktower at the Broadway and waited to cross at the lights. "Maybe I should go round to Jen's right now – y'know, see how she is ... tell her all about what we're doing at the weekend..."

Talk about killing two birds with one stone; I could find out how Jen was really doing *and* get out of going to the square!

"Nice try!" Kyra smirked, linking her arm around mine like a vice and forcibly steering me across Crouch End Broadway, and onwards to the Town Hall. "Look – *I'll* phone Jen tonight and fill her in with what's happening this weekend, so *you* don't have to worry about anything except getting on with The Dare!"

"But what am I supposed to do, Kyra?" I asked her in a panic, as shop windows flew past at high

speed. "Pick out a French lad, and then go up and tell him ... I dunno ... that his skateboard's a nice *colour* or something?!"

"Shut up and stop panicking, Ally!" Kyra said breezily, propelling me on.

"But I don't even know what skateboard is in French!"

"It's *'le skateboard'*, dummy," she tutted. "And you'll think of something better to say than that."

"But Kyra...!"

But nothing. Omigod, we were here ... swivelling to the left round by the telly shop and past the fenced-in section of grass that made up part of the square (or "pigeon park", as Tor liked to call it). Ahead of us, the whole pedestrianized patch outside the old Town Hall was heaving with slouching, chatting, skateboarding people. Good grief – in our prissy school uniforms, me and Kyra were going to stick out like a couple of traffic wardens at an Avril Lavigne concert.

"I don't think I can *do* this..." I mumbled, feeling my legs fill with those mysterious collywobbles, and getting sheer panic blindness from gazing round at such a crowd of hipper-than-me strangers.

"Course you can. Now keep your eyes peeled for any –"

French lads: that's probably what she'd planned

to say, though in my mortified state, I think I'd have rather she'd come up with "any alien spacecraft who will abduct you and therefore save you the embarrassment of making a fool of yourself in front of the whole square".

But she didn't say "French lads", or the stuff about the alien spacecraft. What she *actually* said was: "Course you can. Now keep your eyes peeled for any – *AAAAAEEEEIIIIIIOOOOOUUUUU!!!*"

OK, so it might not have been spelt exactly like all the vowels of the alphabet run together, but it sure sounded like that.

Great. With that one almighty yell, Kyra had made one of my worst nightmares come true: everyone – Highgate Woods kids, random French lads, a few tramps, hundreds of pigeons and most of the queue at the nearby W7 bus stop – had turned to stare at us and see who'd been murdered.

And speaking of murder, I was going to kill Kyra Davies, unless she had a very, *very* good reason for shrieking like that...

HOW NOT TO SPEAK FRENCH, LESSON 1...

"Aaah!"

That wasn't a sigh, by the way, that was more of a sharp intake of breath.

It was 10.15 on Saturday morning, a time when I usually like to be eating large amounts of peanut butter on toast in front of the telly. Instead I had just slithered into the unusually icy depths of the Park Road swimming pool. What was their problem? Had they forgotten to pay their electricity bill and not been able to put the water heater on or something? It might have been all sunshiney outside, but I was going to catch unseasonal frostbite at this rate.

I wasn't the only one; Chloe, Sandie and Kellie were wide-eyed and speechless with the shock of the cold as they bounced in the water beside me, while Salma – hearing our gasps as we plunged in – hadn't got any further than clinging on to the ladder at the edge of the pool and tentatively wafting her toe in.

"Come on, Sal!" Chloe ordered her through

chattering teeth, recovering her voice (just).

Slowly, tentatively, Salma dipped a few more pink-painted toenails under the water. And then Chloe lifted both arms and splashed a deluge of water over her and that was that.

"Thanks a lot!" growled Salma, as she gave in and lowered herself in beside us and all the other mugs who'd come for a morning's swim and were going to go home with hypothermia.

Despite the arctic conditions, the whole pool was heaving, actually. There were heaps of families consisting of millions of little kids shrieking and splashing; there were some old people pootling up and down, doing incredibly slow lengths and tutting at the little kids shrieking and splashing; there were guys showing off doing the butterfly stroke and sending tidal waves over everyone in the process; there was a bunch of office-type girls swimming and chatting and then turning all grouchy 'cause their hair was getting soaked by the butterfly guys' tidal waves; and there was a posse of roaring small boys doing full-on belly flops off the diving boards (ouch, that must hurt).

So yeah, the place was busy. But I'll tell you who *wasn't* there:

1) Kyra. We'd waited outside for ages and then given up on her.

2) Jen. Ditto.

3) Any exchange students. So much for Kellie's hot tip this time. (Course you can guess that I was secretly pleased by this!)

4) Penguins. Which was a shame, really, because they would have found the icy waters a perfect temperature, I think.

"Look, here she is!" Kellie suddenly called out, pointing a dripping, goosebumpy dark arm out of the water in the direction of the tunnel that led from the changing rooms.

I turned to see which missing "she" it was – Kyra or Jen – and saw Kyra sashaying in, wearing a cute little denim-look bikini. If they weren't already frozen, my shoulders would have sunk at the sight of her; I suddenly wished that *I* had a cute little denim-look bikini instead of a boring black school swimming costume that was so old it had wriggly little bits of worn Lycra popping up all over it like tiny fish scales. And I wouldn't have minded having long, skinny, permanently light-brown legs like Kyra's – looking down through the ripples of water at my own legs, all I could see was a pair of milk-white thighs and off-white knobbly knees (the off-white was all that was left of my "glorious" summer "tan").

"Where've you been?" asked Chloe, as Kyra hunkered down at the edge of the pool.

"A girl has to get her beauty sleep," drawled Kyra, but the smirk was quickly wiped from her face when she dipped her ankles into the water.

"You were too lazy to get out of bed, you mean!" laughed Kellie.

"So let's see this terrible wound we've been hearing about then!" Salma demanded, nodding at Kyra's feet.

While we'd been waiting for her outside, I'd kept my friends entertained by telling them about the Town Hall Square disaster yesterday afternoon. That awful, heart-stopping scream that Kyra had come out with? You know what that was all about? It was all because some skateboarder had come zooming past us and clipped her on the ankle. When I say "clipped", it was hardly a case of having a chunk of bone and muscle gouged out, it was more like having a moth's wing brush against your skin. Honestly, the skateboarder boy hardly touched her – there wasn't a scratch or a bruise to be seen, let alone blood and gore. But Kyra being Kyra had to make it sound like she'd been mown down by a runaway juggernaut. I had to endure the shame of bending down and examining her non-injured ankle, before she insisted that we hobble away and get it checked out at her nearby doctor's surgery (the nurse took a look at it and told a

disappointed Kyra that it wasn't even swollen, never mind broken).

Still, enormously embarrassing as it had been, at least I had Kyra's foot to thank for getting me out of The Dare...

"There! *That's* where his board got me!" said Kyra, lifting a leg out of the water and pointing to absolutely nothing on her ankle bone.

Chloe, followed by Salma, swam closer for a better look, but it was all a ruse; before Kyra knew what was happening, Salma and Chloe had reached up, grabbed her arms and hauled her in with an almighty splash.

When she came up spluttering from under the water, Kyra had the same shocked expression on her face as Tor had had last night, when Harry from next door came through and asked us if we'd seen Tabitha, as she'd gone missing. The difference was, as soon as the initial shock wore off, Tor had yelped, "Is it 'cause of Fluffy?" while Kyra had just yelped a very rude word. Loudly.

"Shush, Kyra! You'll get into trouble with the lifeguards if they hear you swearing!" said Sandie, reminding Kyra of one of the no-no rules on a poster hung on the nearby wall.

"Couldn't help it," Kyra frowned, shivering as she bobbed beside us and yanking her bikini top back to

its rightful position. "Anyway, what's the point of us being here? Where are all the French lot?"

"They could still come!" said Kellie defensively, hoping I guess that her gossip network hadn't let her down.

"Anyway, Jen's not here yet," I butted in, now that I was getting slightly acclimatized to my hypothermia and my vocal cords had thawed out. "What did she say when you spoke to her last night?"

"What?" frowned Kyra, beads of water glistening on her black eyelashes.

"What did Jen say when you *phoned* her last night?" I repeated.

Maybe her eardrums – or her brain – had got flooded while she was submerged just now.

"Was I supposed to phone her?"

Oooh, Kyra Davies can be *so* infuriating! *What* had she reassured me she was going to do when we were walking to the Town Hall Square yesterday? Hadn't she *insisted* she'd phone Jen? And didn't I suddenly feel like a total *louse* for not calling Jen myself, and trusting useless Kyra Davies to keep her useless promise?

"Kyra!" I gasped. "You *said* you would – you were supposed to tell her what the plans were for this weekend!"

"Um..."

"You plonker, Kyra!" exclaimed Chloe, splashing water at her in punishment.

"No splashing!" hissed Sandie. "You're not meant to do that either! What if—"

"God, Sandie's right," hissed Kellie. "Here comes a lifeguard now! We're for it! But hold on a sec … isn't he…?"

Kellie couldn't quite figure out why the lifeguard looked so familiar, but I recognized him straight away when he bent down and called me over to the side of the pool.

"Hi, Ally!" grinned Alfie, beaming so wide I caught a glimpse of his gold tooth at the back there.

My worries about Jen would have to keep for a minute or two. My *main* worry right now was choking on the mouthful of water I'd just gulped in at the shock of seeing Alfie out of the blue like this. (Drowning in front of him would be so *deeply* uncool…)

"*Erk*…" I coughed and spluttered, doggy-paddling away from my friends towards him, all the time aware of my face flushing like an inferno (hey, but then it might compensate for the rest of me feeling like an ice-block). "*Erk* … hi! What are you … *erk* … doing here?"

"Working," Alfie shrugged and smiled. "I'm, like, a lifeguard."

"Since … since when?" I blurted out in surprise.

Sure enough – *how* weird – Alfie was wearing a regulation lifeguard outfit of navy T-shirt and tracksuit bottoms, instead of his usual scruffily trendy tops and worn jeans. It was also weird (no – make that *terrifying*) to think that he was seeing me at my very, very worst. Gazing down at me right now, could he see my two-tone white legs and knobbly knees through the ripples of chlorinated water? Could he see that I was so cold that the goosebumps made me look like I had some rare tropical skin disease? Would he maybe think I'd shoved a couple of ice-cubes down the front of my swimsuit, or did he realize they were my own frozen nipples, standing to attention? And – eek! – had he spotted me when I first came out of the changing rooms and hovered for a second, hauling my swimsuit out of my bum before I got in the pool? Oh, the *shame*…!

"I worked outside in the lido all summer!" he informed me, chucking his thumb over his shoulder at the now closed, out-of-season outdoor pool beyond the full-length plate-glass windows. "I stopped once term started again, but … y'know, this guy was off sick today and so they called me and asked me to come in."

Wait a minute – Alfie had been a lifeguard in the

lido the whole summer?! What was going on with the communication in my family? Why had Linn never mentioned it? If I'd known, I'd have dragged my friends here every single day of the summer holidays! I'd have camped out here! I could have bought myself a cute denim-look bikini, got a half-decent tan that didn't give you the cut-off lines that shorts do, and I could have had a legitimate reason to ogle – sorry, hang around Alfie for weeks on end!

Oh, life can be so cruel sometimes…

"Listen … I left a note for Linn last night – y'know, telling her about how I wanted to hang out with her *and* Rowan. I put it through your door about eight-ish. Do you know if she got it?"

Alfie … cheekbones … blondish spiky hair … smiling … talking to me … it was hard not to get completely hypnotized. But if I didn't pull myself together and answer him, he'd think I was quietly demented and never talk to me again.

"Um, yeah … Dad picked it up, so I guess he gave it to her," I told him, remembering the plop! of the letterbox interrupting our family conversation in the living room last night with Harry. Tabitha hadn't come in the night before, he said; she'd never stayed out all night, not at any time during her fifteen-year-old life, he'd said. We all promised to keep our eyes peeled, and then Dad went to check on what had come through the door, just as Harry had thanked us and made moves to leave.

"Great!" grinned Alfie, looking reassured. "Listen, better go – I'm on duty at the diving boards and have to check those little brats don't jump in on top of each other for a laugh..."

"Oh, OK!" I replied, doing some kind of backward doggy paddle as he stood upright and bounded away.

Naturally – totally fazed and humiliated as I was – I didn't look where I was going.

"Uh! *Pardon!*" said someone who I'd just collided with.

The someone had olive skin, intense greeny-brown eyes and darkish, swept-back hair; but then it's always hard to tell what someone's true hair colour and hairstyle is when it's plastered to their head in a swimming pool. The someone also had a purply bruised bump on the bridge of his nose.

"Oh, sorry!" I gasped, flailing around in the water and finding myself practically chest-to-chest with the French boy who Salma had almost brained the day before.

"No problem!"

He was smiling, and he had no clothes on. Well, near enough – you know what I mean. *"Je ne t'ai pas reconnu sans tes vêtements!*" was on the tip of my tongue. Can you imagine if I'd said that out loud? "I didn't recognize you without your clothes on"?! It would have been horrible – I'd have had to drown myself on the spot! Instead, I said...

"Her mum seemed funny there. Didn't she seem funny there? When she let us in just now?"

Me and Sandie, we'd decided to come round to Jen's straight after we'd left the pool. One reason was because we wanted to see how she was (obviously), the second was to try and cheer her up by telling her about the attempt to crash the French crew's leaving party tonight, and the third was to get away from my other friends as fast as I could before they teased me for the fortieth time about my pathetic, failed attempts to do The Dare That Would Not Die.

"I thought she was OK," Sandie whispered in reply, as we waited in the living room till Mrs Hudson got Jen down from her room for us. "Just not very ... *smiley*."

"No ... she wasn't very smiley, was she? Hey – do you think Jen's dad's home? That would be *so* embarrassing, if he came into the room at the same time as Jen's mum or something!"

I could feel my toes curling at the very

awkwardness of it all. I might be all right as an amateur agony aunt to my friends and my sister, but the situation between Jen's parents just made me want to cringe and run away. That's why, I guess, I was really glad to have Sandie here with me. Actually, I'd have probably been too nervous to come here at all, if Sandie hadn't been up for it.

"Do you think Mr Hudson's here?" Sandie hissed, looking panic-stricken. "What if he hears us? Or Mrs Hudson? Quick, Ally – let's talk about something else instead, so we don't get caught!"

Me and Sandie, we were getting just a bit over-twitchy, but changing the subject till Jen appeared seemed like a smart idea. And it was pretty easy to come up with an instant alternative subject...

"'Your nose looks big.' *How* could I have said that to that lad?" I winced, remembering my shameful moment in the pool half an hour before. "I meant 'swollen', not 'big'! I just didn't know how to say that in French!"

"Yeah, but then you didn't say *any* of it in French did you?" Sandie gently pointed out to me.

Shame, shame and triple *shame*...

If it wasn't embarrassing enough to have been spotted in all my unglamorous glory by Alfie, and then doggy-paddled my way into a collision with an innocent French boy who'd already been "assaulted" by one of my friends, everything got a whole lot worse when I swam my way over to my friends and triumphantly pointed out that I'd done The Dare at last during my mini-conversation with the bruised boy. Chloe managed to totally burst my bubble by, in turn, pointing out that I had:

a) spoken to him all right (there was a tick in my favour!)

b) been overheard talking to him by all my mates (another tick!)

c) but had ruined everything by chatting to him entirely in English…

I know – *what* a goofball I am.

"Oh, hi, Jen!" Sandie beamed, as our pale-looking friend finally appeared in the doorway of the living room.

"Hi…" Jen muttered, walking in and slipping silently on to an armchair, like a little, weightless ghost.

And then she said nothing, just gave a little shrug and stared at the floor. This definitely didn't feel right; normally Jen was one of our easiest-to-get-on-with friends. Usually, Jen was always fun, giggling herself silly till the rest of us ended up giggling too. OK, so she'd been a bit blue this week (understandably), but nothing like *this*. What had

changed? Why did it suddenly feel so uncomfortable to be here, and why wasn't Jen even making eye contact with us?

"Are you all right?" I asked the shrunken, huddled-up person who looked a little bit – but not much – like my old mate Jen.

"Mmm," came an unconvincing murmur.

"How come you weren't at sch—"

The start of my question about Jen missing school yesterday coincided with two things: Jen's mum appearing at the door to ask if anyone wanted a juice or anything, and Jen finally raising her gaze from the floor to flash me and Sandie an imploring look that seemed to beg: "Please don't say what you're going to say!"

I didn't know about Sandie, but all I sensed was that not only did Jen want me to shut right up, but also it was a really bad idea to be here at *all*.

"No, thanks!" I heard Sandie answer Mrs Hudson's offer of drinks.

"We just came to let Jen know that we're all meeting at Kellie's tonight at 7.30!" I told Mrs Hudson and Jen all at the same time. I couldn't explain what we were meeting at Kellie's house *for* (i.e. going to go and try to crash the French leaving party straight after), since Mrs Right-on Hudson

might find trailing after boys "demeaning" or something, but I figured we could fill Jen in with the details later.

"Well, that would be fun, wouldn't it!" Jen's mum smiled at her daughter.

Sandie's not a nudger; she doesn't have sharp enough elbows for the job. But she did lean her knee ever so slightly against mine, and I got the message straight away.

"We'd better go!" I said brightly, standing up to leave, with Sandie practically beating me to it.

"See you later, Jen!" she trilled, as we sped towards the front door and escaped from the distinctly weird atmosphere.

"Jen's mum doesn't know she was off school yesterday, does she, Ally?" my best friend whispered as soon as Mrs Hudson had called goodbye and shut the front door behind us.

"Nope," I agreed, feeling my stomach churn into complicated knots.

"What was she doing, if she wasn't at school, and she wasn't at home, Ally?"

Funny Sandie should ask, since that thought was currently burning a hole in my head.

"I don't know," I murmured. "I know she hasn't wanted to talk much about the divorce and stuff, but Jen better tell us tonight what's going on."

If Jen could be trusted not to skive off, just like she had with school, of course...

Chapter 16

ZERO TO NIL CHANCE

Without even checking out the labels on Billy's clothes, I knew they'd be whatever were the hippest names at the moment in the skater magazines he was always poring over in the newsagent's. Oh, yes, from the perfect curve on the peak of his new baseball cap to the tip of his unscuffed best trainers, Billy – my brave, wounded, cat-rescuing hero – had dressed to impress.

And who was he trying to impress? Here's my guess: any French lads who might be even *thinking* of trying to eye up his girlfriend. Speaking of his girlfriend, he was holding on to Sandie's hand so tightly I suspected he might have dribbled a bit of superglue on there, just to be sure...

"We're never going to be able to sneak into the party, not with *you* hanging around, Billy," Chloe informed him huffily, as our little gang left the road that bordered Kellie's council estate and stepped on to the grass that bounded the grounds of Alexandra Palace.

"Chloe, we're never going to be able to sneak into the party *anyway,*" I pointed out, not that Chloe, or any of my other over-excited mates, paid the slightest attention to what I'd just said.

I was kind of bugged by them, if you want to know the truth. When it got to 8 p.m. and it was obvious Jen wasn't going to show up at Kellie's, I'd suggested we phone her, but the others all over-ruled me, reminding me that Jen wanted her space, and that she'd probably phone one of us and talk about stuff when she was good and ready. But you know something? Even if they didn't realize it, I think Kyra and Chloe and Kellie and Salma were all more interested in this potential party than in Jen right at that moment.

And so I found myself trudging on across the grass alongside them all. Slightly to our left, perched high on the hill, Alexandra Palace looked amazing and imposing, with clouds skimming slowly behind it. Meanwhile, directly ahead of us – looking like a glorified public loo – the cricket pavilion squatted in the middle of what used to be a racecourse here, years and years ago.

"Oh, *yewww*!" Kyra grimaced, lifting one foot up from the grass and examining something disgusting on the bottom of her pretty, strappy sandal.

There may not be horses – or horse poo – to

worry about any more in this part of the park, but there were still plenty of dog owners around who didn't pick up after their pooches.

"You'd better get that off," said Chloe, watching as Kyra leant on Kellie for support and frantically brushed her foot back and forth over a patch of fresh grass. "'Cause we'll never be able to sneak in if you've got smelly dog poo on your shoe!"

Chloe really didn't get it – she was still desperately trying to convince herself that all seven of us were going to be able to gatecrash the French crew's leaving do, no problem.

As far as I was concerned, we had zero to nil chance of tiptoeing past the teachers from the French department unseen. We'd have to be suddenly blessed with superhero powers and be able to turn ourselves invisible. And we were definitely not looking invisible at the moment; all my girlfriends had dug out their favourite partying clothes, and from all the sparkly hairclips and spangly bracelets they were wearing, it looked like Salma, Chloe, Kellie and Kyra had bought out the entire stock of Claire's Accessories when they went shopping together in Wood Green this afternoon.

Me, I'd dressed down, only wearing my medium-ly favourite stuff – my fitted purple T-shirt, my jeans with the purply flowers sewn on at the bottom of one leg (hand-me-downs from Rowan – they were too "boring" for her, i.e. perfect for me), and a pair of not-too-scruffy trainers.

Well, what was the point of getting all dressed up, when we'd probably all end up back at Kellie's house in fifteen minutes' time, once we'd been told to get lost by Mr Matthews and co? And as far as I was concerned, that wasn't a bad option; there was quite a good movie on the telly, and Kellie's very generous mum was bound to rustle something up for us all in the kitchen (Mrs Vincent's mission in life was to "feed everyone up!").

Also – and I think you might have guessed this – I was just a tiny-*weeny* bit desperate for us to get turned away from the party. The minute we got shooed off was the minute my troubles were over. If we couldn't get in, then I couldn't do The Dare. And as Kellie didn't have any info on where any of the exchange students would be tomorrow (Sunday), and they were all off on their coach, back home to Whatever-it's-called in Normandy first thing on Monday morning, I'd be officially OFF THE HOOK!!

Joy, joy, joy ... I'd have lost and been the hairy maggot and I didn't *care*.

"Don't worry about *me*, Chloe," said Kyra snippily,

as she checked the sole of her newly cleaned shoe and seemed pleased enough with it. "*You* just worry about checking out the side door!"

"Look, I told you already, I've got it all sussed out! I've been there before when my uncle's football team hired it for a party!" Chloe grouched back.

Ha! So Chloe and Kyra were both nervous about this gatecrashing business – those hints of grumpiness proved *that* all right. You'd never have thought it ten minutes ago, when they were both boasting about how easy it would be to sneak in the side door that Chloe knew about and have all the fun of a party with none of the invite...

"Looks pretty quiet," Kellie pointed out, as we all bounded across the dried-out ditch that circled the immaculate cricket pitch. (Feeling foolishly sorry for Kyra in her heels, I held out my hand and helped her as she teetered her way down into the ditch and scrambled up the other side.)

Actually, what Kellie had just said was true – from where we were standing (waiting for Kyra), the cricket pavilion did look very ... *shut*.

"Course it looks quiet from *this* side! The main entrance is at the back, beside the car park!" Chloe insisted, trudging determinedly onwards across the neatly mown lawns.

Er ... I didn't like to say anything and suffer the wrath of Chloe, but although I couldn't see *all* of it, I could spy a chunk of the car park at that moment, and there wasn't one single car in it. I knew plenty of the exchange students would have walked there, along with their host families, but surely there'd be the odd car there: maybe a parent dropping people off; a teacher's battered Volvo parked up...

Weird.

"So, Chloe, what do we do again when we get to the side door?" Salma asked.

"There'll be loads of people milling about, so we just hover about and chat for a bit, till we cop a good look at what's going on –"

Cop a good look at what, exactly? And which people milling about? The only people I could make out anywhere near the cricket pavilion right now were a couple in football shirts throwing a (very big) stick for their rottweiler.

"– then if everything's OK, I'll nip in the side door and see if the coast is clear, and if there's no teachers around, I'll give you lot the signal and you can sneak in behind me!"

"What if the side door isn't open?" asked Kellie.

"The side door's *always* open!" Chloe said irritably, not wanting to hear anything negative to do with her ace plan.

Again, I wasn't going to contradict her and get my head bitten off, but just 'cause the side door had been propped open the *one* time Chloe had been there, it didn't mean it was exactly a regular occurrence.

"Um, Chloe..." Billy suddenly ventured.

"What?"

"The shutters are down."

Billy's eyes were scrunched up, staring at the building ahead of us.

"What shutters?" Chloe snapped.

"The shutters on the pavilion – they're down."

"So?"

"So that means it's closed!"

He was right. The shutters *were* down, and the pavilion looked about as lively as a funeral director's. If there was a party going on there, it was a pretty quiet one, in the dark.

"Not necessarily!" Chloe barked.

"Uh, *yeah*, necessarily," Billy laughed, which is always a dangerous thing to do when Chloe's got a bit of a temper on her. But instead of turning on Billy, she swivelled her red head round to stare accusingly at Kellie.

"OK, so someone gave me the wrong information!" Kellie shrugged. "But listen – I've got an idea...!"

I didn't care what Kellie's idea was, although I

hoped it involved going back to hers and eating lots of great West Indian food. All I could think about was the fact that no party = no Dare to do.

Yes, yes, *yessssss*!

I didn't get away with it *that* easily, and I didn't get to eat any of Mrs Vincent's cooking either.

Kellie's idea was that maybe her spies had only got the information *half* wrong. Yeah, so the party wasn't at the Ally Pally cricket pavilion; maybe it was at the cricket pavilion near the grounds of Highgate Woods school.

My heart plummeted like it had been dropped off a twenty-storey tower block when she suggested that, but it pinged right back up into its normal resting place half an hour later, when we shipped up to the other pavilion and heard party music spilling out of the open doors.

"Isn't that like a *waltz* or something?" Kyra had said, wrinkling up her nose in disgust.

Yes it was, and hurrah! we'd found a party all right, but it was some kind of old people's knees-up, with not a French exchange student in sight.

It had been hard to look as disappointed as everyone else at that point, but I'd managed to grumble "S'pose so!" when Chloe suggested we just all give up and go home.

And so here I was, bounding up to my front gate, with not a care in the world now that the weight of The Dare was off my shoulders. I planned to celebrate by putting on a CD really loud, and dancing like a freak around my bedroom till I got dizzy. (That's *if* my dad had got round to fixing my door back on, of course.) And maybe I should give Jen a phone too...

"Hi, Ro!" I grinned a Cheshire cat grin in my sister's direction, as she came out the front door in a flurry of velvet and sparkles. The velvet was a loose, short patchwork dress she'd made out of a bunch of second-hand cushion covers she'd picked up at a jumble sale; the sparkles were these tiny twinkly plastic clips she'd pinned all over the tangles of dark ringlets she had twisted her hair into tonight. As the sun went down, it would look like a bunch of fireflies had landed on her head.

"Hi, Ally," she replied kind of flatly, stuffing her keys into one of the many pockets on her army-style canvas bag.

"Are you going to meet Alfie?" I asked her, pausing and holding the gate open for her with my bum.

"Yeah, but..."

"Hold on – you've got something on your sleeve," I pointed out, stopping her and scraping at

something pinkish on the sleeve of the white long-sleeved top she was wearing under her home-made dress.

"It's clay – Mum's dug out all her old pottery stuff from the attic cupboard and started making … a thing."

My heart soared and I immediately stopped picking at the dried-in clay grains with my fingernail.

"That's brilliant!" I beamed at Rowan.

Mum making, well, *things* – that was just like old times. It felt like being time-machined back into my childhood, when the house was always full of half-finished paintings and sculptures and general arty-fartyness. Mum never seemed to mind that all of us got muddled about what her stuff was meant to be. She didn't care that Linn thought her painting of a sunset was of a fried egg, or that Grandma once put a driftwood mobile she'd just finished making in the bin 'cause she thought it was rubbish. (I mean, she thought that the *driftwood* was rubbish, not Mum's mobile. Er, then again…)

"Mmm," nodded Rowan, agreeing with me by giving a watery little smile. Which happened to match her watery little eyes…

"What's up?" I asked, feeling warm swirls of

happiness fade instantly away at the sight of Rowan's smudged mascara.

"Linn."

"What's she done now?"

"I just heard her on the phone to her friend Mary, making plans for Alfie's birthday tomorrow. She knew I could hear her, so she just started talking louder – you know, just to rub it in that I'm not allowed to be there!"

Help … *that* didn't sound good. So much for my note-writing tip – Linn must have read what Alfie wrote to her by now … and ignored it.

"You know what she's like," I shrugged, not really knowing what to say. "Just forget about her and have a nice time with Alfie tonight."

"But that's just it, Ally," Ro said wearily. "I'm thinking of chucking him."

"What?!" I squawked. How could any girl lucky enough to date Alfie be so insane as to let him go?

"It's too *hard*, Ally! All this stuff with Linn and everything, it's upsetting Alfie, I *know* it. Maybe it would be easier for them to just be friends again, and if I finish with him, maybe she'll be less horrible to me…"

"Don't be silly! You can't chuck Alfie just 'cause Linn hasn't got used to the idea of you two going out together yet! You've got to give it time!"

God, I sounded like Mum giving Tor the talk about Tabitha and Fluffy.

"I dunno..." mumbled Rowan, shaking her head sadly and making her hairclips spangle dots of lights in my eyes. "Look, I better go or I'll be late..."

I watched Rowan for a second, as she hurried off, spangles bouncing, even if her spirit wasn't. Then I mooched inside, hoping I wouldn't bump into Linn, since she wasn't exactly my favourite sister right now. I mean, how could she be so mean to Rowan after Alfie had written her that letter? I never saw what he wrote, but was she really so hard-hearted that she could just ignore what her best mate had to say?

"Hi, Ally Pally!" Dad smiled up at me from the armchair as I hovered in the living-room doorway. "Did you see Rowan, just now? She just went out."

"Yeah, I did. Where's everyone else?" I asked, referring to the humans in our family, since plenty of the animal members were visible, curled up or flopped out around the room.

"Tor and Ivy are in bed, Linn's in her room," Dad began to tell me, as I walked over to him and sat down on the arm of his chair, "and Mum's in the shower washing clay out of her hair, I think."

"Did you manage to fix my door?" I asked, not

that I was in the mood to blast my CDs and dance around my room like a freak any more.

"Oh, God – sorry, Ally! I totally forgot! What an idiot!"

Dad had been pretty forgetful recently, but it wasn't 'cause he was going prematurely senile, I don't think – I guess it had more to do with his brain being a bit scrambled with happiness ever since Mum had come back for good.

"And that's just reminded me of something else I forgot," he said, slapping his forehead. "Sandie phoned for you about five minutes ago – she sounded a bit upset. Something about Kyra saying something to Billy that she shouldn't have about a boy at the ice rink or something?! Does that make any sense?"

Uh-oh, I'd only left my friends ten minutes ago, and it seemed like I'd missed some drama.

"Kind of. I'd better go and see what the emergency is," I told him, pushing myself up off the chair.

And then my eyes caught a glimpse of a corner of an envelope on the floor, sticking out from under yesterday's paper, which in turn was underneath a snoozing cat that wasn't Colin.

"What's that?" I asked, touching it with the toe of my trainer.

Dad frowned and reached down ... and pulled

out an envelope with "Linn" written on it.

"What's wrong with my brain? Maybe it needs oiling!" Dad joked, staring at the envelope. "I meant to leave this on the kitchen table for Linn after Harry left last night, but I must have put it down with the paper and just forgot."

So Linn *hadn't* read Alfie's letter – well, that explained something.

"I'll take it up to her now," I suggested, letting Dad pass it to me.

Hurtling up the stairs two at a time, I just hoped it wasn't too late to make a difference. I just hoped Rowan wasn't out there right now, making a huge mistake and finishing with Alfie.

"Good luck!" I whispered to the envelope, as I gently shoved it under Linn's door – then knocked and ran away *fast*...

OINK

Sometimes, when you're blue, there's only one thing to do to cheer yourself up – stroke a pig.

Well, that's what you do when you're Tor, anyway. If you're Sandie, you buy three bars of chocolate and eat them all at once.

It was 10 a.m. on Sunday morning, and I was being an excellent sister and excellent best friend at the same time. Last night, Mum and Dad were telling me how upset Tor was at Tabitha's mysterious disappearance, so straight away I decided to take him (and Ivy of course) to the City Farm in nearby Holloway as a cheer-up treat. That meant I'd had to phone Billy and cancel our regular Sunday morning dog-walking session, which in turn meant I got to hear Billy's version of what happened after I'd left my friends outside the second, *wrong*, cricket pavilion last night. I'd already heard Sandie's version – I'd called her back right after I'd stuck Alfie's note under Linn's door (and run away).

Both versions amounted to the same thing, which was:

• Seconds after I'd walked away, Salma suggested that they all go up to the ice rink, on the off chance that some of the exchange students would be hanging out there again.

• Kyra said that was a good idea, as it had been such a laugh when they all went last time, and "wasn't it funny when the va-va-va voom boy waved at Sandie and she went all shy?".

• Kyra realized what she'd said and slapped her hand over her mouth.

• Billy and Sandie went off and had a fight.

All that stuff sounded the same in *both* their versions, but in Sandie's it ended with her apologizing for not telling him, and in Billy's it ended with him imagining that Sandie was secretly in love with the "voo-voo" boy and planning to run off to Normandy to be with him for ever and ever and ever.

Tor, Rowan, Linn, Alfie, Billy, Sandie … it had been an exhausting Saturday night of listening, sorting and fixing for Ally the amateur agony aunt. In fact, it had been so busy that I hadn't had a second to call Jen. Still, I'd make up for that and call her at lunchtime, when I got home. And at the same time, I might get a better idea of what was

going on with my sisters: neither of them had been up by the time me, Tor and Ivy had headed off this morning. So what had happened last night with Rowan and Alfie, I wondered? Had she (eek) finished with him? And what about Linn and the letter? She'd stayed in her room last night, so I hadn't had a chance to study her; to see if anything in her face gave away her reaction to Alfie's letter…

"But I tried to *tell* Billy; I tried to tell him nothing's going on with me and SF!" Sandie insisted, as we went to follow Ivy and Tor into the barn. "And all he said was, 'Oh, how *cosy* – you've got your own nickname for that guy now!'"

Sandie had wanted to talk everything over with me, and I'd wanted to take Tor out, so we'd combined the girly chat with the outing to the farm.

"*I* told him nothing was going on too, but you can't blame him for being hurt!" I shrugged. "It's just that you didn't mention going to the ice rink the other day, so it came across like you were keeping some big secret from him."

"I know … I *know* it's all my fault. What am I going to do, Ally?"

Ally the amateur agony aunt was in business again. I couldn't think up a sensible answer for

Sandie straight away, but I came up with something that might help in the meantime.

"I'd get more chocolate if I was you," I told her, giving a nod in the direction of the small farm shop. So what if she'd already eaten an Aero, a Kit-Kat and a Lion bar on the bus over here; it was all medicinal.

"Yeah, I think I will..." mumbled Sandie sadly, as she drifted off.

"I'll stay here with the kids!" I called after her. "Get Ivy a carton of juice, will you?"

Sandie didn't hear that last bit; one of the cockerels strutting around had a voice that was nearly as loud as Chloe's mum, and his sudden crowing totally drowned my words out.

And so I gave up and marched into the barn after my kid brother and sister. Apart from cheering Tor up, I was dying to see Ivy's face when she caught a close-up glimpse of the goats and sheep and cows in this place.

Tor, of course, had led her to his favourite animal at the City Farm. At the far end of the barn, he was leaning his arm through some railings, scratching a head that I couldn't quite see yet but that I knew belonged to Tina the pig. It seemed that Ivy couldn't quite see her either – she was standing on her tiptoes, clutching her pink teddy

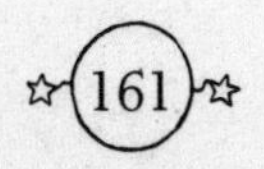

under one arm and Mr Penguin under the other, teetering around on the straw-covered ground.

"Hold on," I told her, scooping her up so that she could put her pink-wellied feet on one bar of the fence surrounding Tina's pen.

"Hello, pretty piggy!" she beamed, gazing down at a fat, snorting face that wasn't destined to win a beauty contest any time soon.

"What does the pig say, Ivy?" I asked her.

She didn't answer me, but that wasn't any big surprise. Like her big brother Tor, Ivy is kind of the *opposite* of a chatterbox. (Do they have a word for that? And who are "they" anyway?)

"Oink!" I answered for her, which got her giggling.

The thing with kids is, once you get them laughing, it's so cute you want to do it some more.

"Oink! Oink!"

Now Tor was sniggering too, and even Tina seemed interested in what I had to say, judging from the way she was squinting her beady eyes at me.

"Oink, oink, oink, oink!"

"Uh, hello…"

For a second it was just like a moment from *Babe* the movie, with the little piggy chattering away in human-ese. But then if Tina really *had*

wanted to start up a conversation with me in my language, I suspected she'd have sounded like a girl, and not a boy. And I didn't suppose she'd have had a French accent…

"Er, hi…" I mumbled, half-hiding behind Ivy so that the boy with the bump on his nose – i.e. the lad I'd crashed into at the pool yesterday – couldn't get a good look at the blush on my face.

"This is your family?" he asked, pointing to Tor and Ivy, who stared curiously back at him.

"Yes – that's my brother and this is my little sister," I told him.

"That is my family there." He pointed in the direction of a guy I recognized from the year above me, a set of parents and some little kids over by the donkeys. "Not mine, I mean – the family that I am staying with!"

I laughed, a bit too loud 'cause I was nervous, but luckily, the boy laughed too. And then we both went quiet, not really sure what to say.

"What happened to your nose?" Tor piped up, in the vacuum.

"I had a fight – with a door!"

I liked this boy. He made jokes (sort of), and got Tor giggling. And he didn't seem to hold a grudge against me for having a friend who was clumsy enough to slam big chunks of wood in his face.

"Stéphane! We're leaving *nowwwww*!" called the woman over by the donkeys, picking up one whiny, grizzly kid. The lad I recognized from the year above me looked bored rigid. I guess he'd have preferred to be playing PlayStation 2 in his room with "Stéphane", rather than be press-ganged into this corny family outing.

"OK, I must go," said Stéphane, shooting me a smile. "I hope you have fun talking to the pig again!"

I felt the blush flood my cheeks even more – he was teasing me! And it was sort of nice…

"*Au revoir!*"

"*Au revoir*…" I mumbled in reply, as he darted off.

And then something occurred to me.

"Why are you smiling, Ally?" Tor asked, gazing up at me.

"Because I just spoke French! To a boy!" I told him excitedly, although The Dare meant diddlysquat to my little brother.

Yippeeee! I'd done it! Just when I wasn't looking, it had all happened, out of the blue, just like that! I felt like jumping up and down and yelling, "I'VE DONE THE DARE!!" at the top of my voice!

"Anybody want one?" came Sandie's voice, as she walked up to us, rustling a bag of Maltesers.

Ah … once again, I'd forgotten a vital part of The Dare, hadn't I? The part about one of my mates having to be a witness?

Drat, drat and double drat with chocolate on top.

"Oh, hold on … that's mine!"

I don't know why Sandie felt the need to say "That's mine!" when her mobile phone started ringing – *I* certainly didn't have a mobile, and neither did Tor, Ivy, or even Tina the pig, as far as I could make out.

"Maybe it's Billy!" Sandie gushed to me, scrabbling for her phone so madly that she sent precious Maltesers flying.

"Oink!" squeaked Ivy, better late than never, smiling into my face while an expectant Sandie took her call.

"Oink!" I oinked back at Ivy, then sneaked a peek in Sandie's direction, to see if all was well; if she was smiling and making up with her "baby bear". (Urgh … the very thought of her calling Billy her "baby bear" made me feel slightly queasy…)

But Sandie wasn't smiling. She was shaking. She was listening to someone saying something, and she was *shaking*.

Uh-oh…

"It's – it's –"

As I hurried towards her, Sandie was struggling to speak; she helplessly held out her mobile to me, her big blue eyes enormous with panic.

"Hello?" I garbled into the phone.

Who was calling Sandie? *Was* it Billy? Had he just chucked her or something?

"Is that Ally?" came a voice that was vaguely familiar, but certainly didn't belong to Billy.

"Yes..." I replied warily, frantically trying to place the mystery voice.

"This is Jen's mum. Ally – Jen's gone missing..."

I think Sandie started to say something, and I was vaguely aware of the cockerel starting to shrill again, but I couldn't make sense of any normal sounds.

All I could make out was this guilty voice whispering in my head, *"You should have phoned her, Ally... You could have made a difference, Ally... This is your fault, Ally..."*

THE VANISHING TRICK

Last night – somewhere in Crouch End – the French exchange students and the people they'd been staying with had had themselves an excellent leaving party. It was a mystery to me and my party-dressed mates exactly *where* that excellent party might have been.

On the flipside of things, at some point last night, our friend Jen had been *so* miserable that she'd sneaked out of her house, without anyone realizing till morning that her bed hadn't been slept in. Just like the exchange student party, Jen's disappearance was a mystery to us, her mates. The only difference was that not finding a party was mildly disappointing; not knowing where your run-away friend had vanished to was gut-wrenchingly, head-swirlingly *awful*...

"Yappity-yappity-yappity-yap!"

A specially trained sniffer dog, like a police dog or something, might have come in handy for tracking Jen. Or maybe one of those amazing

collies that you see scampering up snow-covered peaks with mountain rescue people. None of my three goofy dogs would be any good at helping in the search for our missing mate, which is why I'd left them at home, when I rushed back there to drop Tor and Ivy off half an hour ago.

"*Yappity-yappity-yappity-yap!*"

So why Billy had thought it would be an excellent idea to take his small, annoying, LOUD, white poodle along with him, I had no idea.

"*Yappity-yappity-yappity-yap!*"

"Oh, *I* see, Sandie. *I* get it. Was this *your* idea, was it, that we should look for Jen here?! Well, isn't that *nice*!"

Kyra being sarcastic: that was normal. Chloe being sarcastic: second nature. Even *I* could do sarcastic pretty well. But Billy coming across all sarcastic? That wasn't too nice at all.

"Billy! It was *not* my idea to look for Jen here!" Sandie protested. "Ally phoned Chloe and the others, and they all decided to split up and look in different areas!"

"Yeah, but I bet *you* suggested looking here," Billy pushed the point again, standing with his hands fist-first in his pockets, staring around the boating lake at Alexandra Palace, at the copious number of French exchange students who were either out on the pedalos, or standing around chatting and eating Cornettos, or feeding their Cornettos to the pushy Canada geese who nested around the boating lake and cheerfully bullied passers-by for any nibbles they'd like to donate to the Fat And Happy Canada Geese Society.

"I did *not*!" Sandie blinked furiously at her supposed boyfriend. "How could I have known they'd be here?"

Billy didn't even look at her; instead he glared off into the distance, hands still rammed in his pockets, Precious the poodle still yapping pointlessly at the end of his lead.

"Sandie *didn't* suggest coming here," I tried to butt in, wishing now that I hadn't phoned Billy in a moment of panic and asked him to help in our search for Jen. If my two so-called best mates could stop fighting for five seconds (and Precious could stop yapping), I might be able to think straight and figure out where in Ally Pally park we should start searching next.

"Yeah? Well it seems a pretty weird coincidence that *he's* here, then!" snapped Billy, nodding his head sharply in the direction of SF, who was loitering over by the boat hire bloke, with a group of friends, eating ice-cream and waiting for a turn on the pedalos.

"Billy, I *told* you," I said wearily, feeling my nerves stretched so tight that I could just about imagine myself bodily *ping*ing all the way across the boating lake and the children's playground, if someone wound me up one *tiny* bit more.

"Told me what?" asked Billy, his eyes wild, but his bottom lip wobbling precariously.

"I *told* you that Chloe and Kellie are looking for Jen in Wood Green, Kyra and Salma are looking in Priory Park and around Crouch End Broadway, and me, Sandie and you are covering Ally Pally."

I was trying *really* hard not to lose my temper. Not only were my friends out searching for Jen, but Jen's sister Rachel was scouring Muswell Hill, and Jen's dad was down at Finsbury Park, checking out the Tube station. Even Linn and Rowan – unbelievably – had offered to go for a wander around Highgate Woods and Queen's Woods (together!), just in case.

Jen's mum, meanwhile, was staying at home, waiting and hoping that someone, *anyone* would call and tell her that Jen was OK...

"Well, I want to find Jen too," Billy announced, "but I don't see why we couldn't have looked in Priory Park or Wood Green or wherever, instead of *here*!"

"Billy – zip it," I warned him, thinking about

inflicting a stinging finger-flick on his scratched chest to shut him up. (Violence was a last resort, I promise!)

"Well, she's not here, is she?" he replied defensively, referring, I supposed, to Jen.

"Fine! Let's go check out the ice rink next!" I suggested, stomping off towards the east entrance to Ally Pally before I lost my temper. A tight-lipped Sandie scampered to be by my side, while a bad-tempered Billy trailed behind, hissing, "Precious, c'mon, boy! Leave that duck alone!"

Y'know, it was strange, barging past all these people who my friends had been desperate to hang out with all week, and who I'd been so nervous of approaching. But right now, knowing Jen was out there somewhere, alone and maybe scared, I couldn't have given a damn about The Dare, or the slightest thing to do with the exchange students.

"Uh ... hi, hello again!"

What happened next was one of those freeze-frame scenes: I hadn't spotted Stéphane before, but now here he was, breaking away from the waiting queue for the pedalos, ice-cream in hand, bruise still visible on his nose, a big friendly smile on his face.

Next thing, the bruise on the bridge of

Stéphane's nose was nowhere to be seen, mainly because he was now *wearing* his ice-cream cone on his face, all thanks to Billy reaching over and shoving it there.

Sandie froze by my side, slapping her hands over her stunned face.

"Billy!" I screeched. "What did you do *that* for!"

Instantly, Stéphane was surrounded by laughing, teasing friends, including SF and the Palace Gates pupil I'd seen Stéphane with at the City Farm this morning.

"Oi!" roared the boy I knew from the year above us. "What's that all about?"

Even though my own question hadn't been answered, all I knew for sure was that I had to get my idiot friend out of there as fast as I could.

"I'm sorry!" I called out in Stéphane's approximate direction, as I hustled Billy and Precious out of the boating lake gate and towards Ally Pally ice rink, with Sandie scurrying behind.

"I thought … I thought he was flirting with Sandie too!" Billy blurted out as I sped him on, now suddenly realizing that maybe, *possibly* he'd made a terrible mistake.

"Billy – he was talking to *me*. Not to Sandie – to *me*," I growled, aware that a potentially interesting friendship/flirtation/whatever had come and gone

in a nanosecond, thanks to a) Billy, and b) a wrongly positioned ice-cream.

"God, I'm so sorry, Ally!" Billy said imploringly.

At least, I *think* that's what he was saying; Precious's demented yappity-yapping practically drowned him out.

I knew then that I was crying; not 'cause of my missed opportunity with Stéphane, or the embarrassment I'd forever suffer at school because of Billy (wrongly) ramming an ice-cream in Stéphane's face – but because we'd just reached a viewpoint of the whole of London stretching out before us.

And somewhere out there – in this huge city – Jen was lost and lonely and alone...

Chapter 19

STRESS, SHIVERING AND STRANGE SCRABBLINGS...

I couldn't imagine what Jen must be feeling, being out all night. Had she managed to sleep at all, wherever she was? Or had she sat up, awake and cold, through the darkness and into the dawn?

As for me, it was only about 1 p.m. on Sunday afternoon, but I suddenly felt as drained as if I'd run three marathons back-to-back, wearing a suit of armour filled with sludge. But I couldn't rest; not while Jen was still missing. The only reason I'd come back home was because Mum had called me on Sandie's mobile and promised that she and Dad would help me search some more this afternoon, if I only came back for some lunch and a break first.

The idea of Mum and Dad helping was great – Sandie and Billy were doing my head in with their bickering. Searching for Jen was stressful enough without them sniping at each other, not to mention making me the future laughing stock of school by smearing ice-cream in an innocent boy's face...

"Oh, Ally!" said Dad, putting the hall phone down as I bumbled in through the front door.

The fact that my dad had just been on the phone made my heart go *ping!* with hope; had he heard something? Then he seemed to clock what I was thinking, and hurried to say: "That was Jen's mum – just to let us know that there's no news of her yet."

"But you know what they say, Ally," Mum tried to reassure me, appearing from the kitchen, "no news is good news!"

No news is good news ... well, *that* was a joke.

"But Jen could be hurt or anything!" I blurted out.

"Don't think like that, Ally," said Mum soothingly, wrapping a comforting arm around me. "Anyway, Mrs Hudson has phoned around the local hospitals and no one who matches Jen's description has been brought in, which is ... a good sign."

But that didn't sound like a good sign to me – not when I suddenly found myself imagining Jen stone-cold dead of hypothermia after a night trying to sleep out in Queen's Woods with only a couple of leaves and a twig to cover her...

"She's shivering..." I vaguely heard Mum tell Dad. "You take her out in the garden and I'll get her a hot drink."

And so a blurry few minutes later, I found

myself sitting in a deckchair in the blazing late summer sunshine, with a wintry mug of hot chocolate clutched in my hands, and a hot, hairy dog's head resting on my feet (Winslet's attempt at comfort, I liked to think).

While Mum clattered around in the kitchen – making a lunch I probably wouldn't be able to eat – Dad sat on the grass beside me, doing his best to cheer me up. Fresh back from their trudge around the woods, Linn and Rowan were busy keeping Tor and Ivy amused, taking turns at pushing the swing that our kid brother and sister were currently sharing, their small bottoms squished next to each other on the red plastic seat. Rolf and Ben were going crazy chasing the swing, missing getting their cold, wet noses bashed by just millimetres.

"OK, so here's the plan, Ally Pally," said Dad matter-of-factly. "After lunch, we'll phone around your friends and see how everyone's got on. Then we'll see if anyone else's parents can help out, and we'll organize bigger search parties. How about that?"

I *was* listening to Dad, but my head was whirring with so many thoughts and possibilities that it was hard to concentrate on his exact words. Instead, I found myself watching Winslet, who'd just sat up all of a sudden, stuck one hairy ear up, scratched it

with her back leg, then wandered off. So much for showing me support – my feet had only been a comfy snooze spot for her.

Gee, thanks! I couldn't help thinking, as Winslet waddled off up the garden. She seemed to be headed in the direction of the shed, where a cat that wasn't Colin – Fluffy to be precise – was currently giving herself a manicure by scratching her claws on the wooden door.

"What do you think, Ally?"

I thought that Fluffy was acting weird, actually. She wasn't so much scratching as *scrabbling*, and making some strange little yowling sound that was clearly confusing Winslet.

"So? Do you think that's a good plan?" I heard Dad's voice ask.

I was just about to answer him when I stopped and frowned. OK, so Fluffy was acting weird, but what on earth was that hairy mutt up to? Winslet was now frantically sniffing around the door as if it held special smelly secrets, and pawing at the wood as if she was trying to copy Fluffy. I wasn't the only one who'd noticed the odd behaviour going on; Tor had just hopped off the swing and gone to investigate.

"What're they all so interested in?" I asked, noticing that Rolf and Ben had also deserted the

swing and had joined in with Winslet and Fluffy's scratch-and-sniff game.

"Dumb dogs," said Dad affectionately. "They must think there's a bone in there..."

Yeah, but Fluffy wouldn't be going that demented over a bone (a tin of Felix, maybe). And I didn't know Ben well enough yet, but I knew for sure that our other two dogs weren't dumb. OK, so Rolf liked to eat polystyrene sometimes and Winslet growled at dust, but deep down they were smart. They had special powers that we supposedly clever humans didn't have: they could hear a packet of turkey slices being opened from three floors away; they could tell a mean dog from a friendly dog in the park, when they all looked cute and fluffy to us; they knew when the heating was about to come on in the winter and settled themselves on the exact spots on the floor where the pipes under the floorboards were about to gurgle hot water through, any minute; wherever it was hidden, no matter how cleverly it was hidden, they could sniff out food ... *and* trouble.

"What? What's wrong?" I called out, wriggling myself out of the slouchy deckchair and hurrying over to the shed.

"Ally...?" Dad's voice trailed after me.

But I didn't turn round. You know how you pick

up people's traits, or even accents, if you hang out with them long enough? Well, maybe it works with animals too. Maybe if you spend enough time with them, some of their special powers rub off on *you*. Maybe I'd just tuned in with the dogs, sensing what *they* were sensing. Then again, I could just be going completely mad…

"They know something, Ally!" said Tor, his eyes wide with alarm as I rushed towards him and our loopy dogs and cat, who were now faintly hysterical and barking and yowling the place down.

"I know – hold on!" I told Tor. "Help me get them out of the way for a sec!"

Gently pushing our pets' combined furry weight off the shed door, I finally managed to yank at the metal clasp and tug the door open. And then … and then…

"Miaow!" miaowed Tabitha, looking dishevelled and tangled but very happy to see me.

So did the dishevelled-looking person whose lap she'd been sitting on.

"Jen…?"

SAFE AND SOUND (PHEW!)

"Ally!" squeaked Jen, untangling her crossed legs and hurtling towards me.

Rushing forward, I gave my not-very-long-lost friend a rib-crunching cuddle.

"Where have you been?" I asked her, letting go just enough to take a look at her and laughing with relief.

"In your shed?" Jen replied sheepishly, blinking her button eyes at me, and smiling a wobbly smile that was just wide enough to show a glimpse of her brace.

All around us was a commotion of voices and barking and people patting Jen. I heard Dad ask Jen if she was OK, then he yelled for Mum and said something about going and phoning Mrs Hudson straight away.

"How long have you been in there?" asked Linn, gently propelling Jen and me – still hugging – away from the shed and towards the house.

Now I could see Mum hurrying out of the back

door towards us, just as Dad hurried inside. Rowan – kneeling beside Tor and Ivy and a madly purring Tabitha – was staring intently at Jen, as if she was a newly landed alien. Fluffy seemed to be doing the same thing to Tabitha, sniffing curiously at her, as if she was some exotic specimen of cat-ness, and not next-door's moggy that she usually couldn't stand.

"I dunno..." Jen shook her head at Linn's question, clearly disorientated.

"What happened, Jen, love? We know you were missing all night..."

Now it was Mum's turn to ask the questions, as she took over from Linn to steer Jen towards the back door.

"Well ... I sneaked out of my house once everyone had gone to bed – it was after midnight, I think," Jen answered her, with all of us hanging on her every word. "But then I didn't know where to go... I just wandered around the streets for ages, trying to decide what to do. And then I got kind of cold and scared, and ... and I just thought of your shed, and knew if I could just hide out in there for a while..."

I guess I could get my head around that: since our shed doubles up as an animal hospital, there's a certain comfort factor to it, unlike normal sheds that are full of dangerously sharp, pointy garden implements and packets of toxic things that are dangerous to kids and pets as well as moss or whatever.

"But why didn't you come out of the shed earlier, Jen?" asked Linn, stepping aside to let Mum, Jen and me go in the back door first. "You must have heard all the racket we were making playing on the swing with the kids!"

"Yeah, I heard," mumbled Jen, dropping her gaze to the floor. "I was too scared to come out… I thought everyone would be … *angry* with me!"

"Oh, Jen, sweetheart…" Mum sighed, pulling up a chair and lowering my friend down on to it, as if she was a fragile, porcelain doll. "No one's going to be angry with you!"

How spooky was *that* to hear – it was only a couple of weeks ago that Mum had explained to us that the main reason *she'd* stayed away from home so long was 'cause she was scared we'd all be angry with her for disappearing on us.

Mum might have hidden away in Cornwall for four years, while Jen had only hidden away in our shed for one night, but it looked like my mum and my friend had an awful lot in common…

It turned out that our unlocked garden shed hadn't

been empty when Jen had sneaked into it in the middle of the night: at first she thought one of our pets must be in quarantine, but soon a shaft of moonlight shining through the window illuminated Tabitha's tangled white fur. Who knows how long Tabitha had been stuck in there (it seemed like quite a while from the way she started devouring Jen's biscuit supply), but Jen was too lonely to open the door and set her free.

Instead, the two of them curled up together and managed to drop off into a dead-to-the-world sleep, snoozling for hours and hours till the sound of voices in the garden had woken them up.

Mum and me got to hear this chunk of Jen's story once the rest of my family had tactfully pootled off to other parts of the house, leaving us and Jen alone in the kitchen to talk. And eat, as it happened.

"Another sandwich, Jen?"

"No thank you, Mrs Love. But could I have some more juice, please?"

"No problem," smiled Mum, getting up and grabbing a fresh carton of orange out of the fridge.

Running away from home is a thirsty business. In the last five minutes, Jen had already drunk a whole carton to herself. Running away must also make you work up quite an appetite, especially

when the only supplies you run away with consist of half a dozen wheat-free oatmeal cookies, pinched from the kitchen cupboard. No wonder Jen had managed to wolf down two cheese and pickle sandwiches and a packet of crisps so far.

"How long were you planning on hiding out in the shed?" I asked Jen, resting my freaked-out head on my hands and staring across the kitchen table at her. Alongside the relief of seeing Jen alive and well and in one glorious (if slightly scruffy) piece, there were a million questions battling for space in my brain, and right now I was trying like mad to assemble them into something that made sense.

"Not much longer – I really, *really* needed a wee," Jen admitted.

That much was obvious. Jen was in the loo for ages; Dad had already finished talking to her extremely relieved mum by the time she finally came down the stairs.

"I know your parents are splitting up, Jen, and that can't be easy. But what made you think about leaving home?" Mum asked gently, smoothing down Jen's sticky-up hair as she refilled her glass with juice.

Now *that* – that was the main question I wanted to know the answer to.

"I just felt ... *miserable,*" Jen blinked at Mum,

dark circles under her dark button eyes. "I didn't want to be in our house any more, not with the weird atmosphere there."

"Has there been a lot of shouting going on?"

"No," Jen shook her head at Mum. "Nobody's been saying *anything*; just crying."

"Your mum?"

"And my sister. But if they see I'm watching they just go in their rooms and cry."

"What about your dad?" Mum suggested. "Have you been able to talk to him?"

"No," Jen shook her head again. "Dad didn't even say goodbye when he moved out – I went home sick from school on Wednesday and he'd just packed a bag and gone. That's when Mum and Rachel started crying all the time. Being at home was horrible, so I just wanted to get away from it."

Wow – I'd no idea that Jen's dad had moved out already. She'd kept *that* to herself. In fact, she'd kept an awful *lot* to herself over the last week. I know that's the way Jen had said she wanted it, but now I felt like a truly lousy friend. So much for thinking of myself as some kind of agony aunt; I should have kept asking her how she was, or even maybe talked to her more about other stuff, just to give her the chance to open up if she'd felt like it. Instead, I'd kept my distance, even though I knew

Jen was going through a rough time. Maybe I could have taken my own advice and written to her; I could've sent her a cute card, with a note inside telling her how sorry I was, and that she could come and talk to me any time…

But there was no time for could'ves and should'ves right now – there were still some questions I wanted to ask her, just to help me understand properly what had gone on.

"You told your mum you were going to Chloe's on Thursday night – but that wasn't true, was it?"

"No. I went and sat on the swings in Priory Park till it got dark."

"And you weren't in school on Friday," I pointed out, remembering the look of alarm on Jen's face, when she thought I was going to blurt that out in front of Mrs Hudson.

"Well, I *was* on my way to school. But then I just … jumped on a bus and ended up taking the Tube to the West End. I hung around Covent Garden all day and then came home at night."

"But why did you want to be on your own? Why didn't you come and talk to me or Kellie or someone if you were unhappy?" I asked her, hurt that she hadn't trusted me or any of our other friends with her problems, even though I knew now that was partly our fault.

"It's because Jen was feeling *more* than unhappy, Ally – she was a bit depressed. And when you're depressed, you don't think straight," Mum chipped in. "Right, Jen?"

Jen gave Mum a nod, listening intently to her.

"All you want to do is get away from the hassles, but really, the hassles are in your head, so running away just makes things worse – and *I* know that more than anyone," Mum continued. "The only way to start feeling better is to talk a lot about how you're feeling, and not bottle it up. I wish I'd done that a long time ago, Jen, 'cause then I might have been back home with my family a lot sooner..."

Mum stretched both her hands out across the table, one of them reaching out to Jen, the other to me. From the watery eyes all three of us had, I think we were in desperate need of a family-sized box of Kleenex.

"My mum is going to be *so* angry with me for running away..." Jen suddenly mumbled, with a distinctly wobbly bottom lip.

"No, she's not," Mum smiled at her. "She's going to give you the biggest hug you've ever had, I guarantee it!"

Jen started to laugh at that, even though tears were trickling down her cheeks.

"That'll be your mum now!" I announced,

jumping up from the table at the sound of the doorbell.

Hurrying through the hallway, I dabbed at my damp eyes with the sleeve of my denim shirt. The worry of Jen being missing, the relief of her turning up, the weirdness of hearing Mum talk the way she just had … it had really given me a bad case of the wibbles.

"Hi, Ally! Is your friend still here? The one who found Tabitha?"

It wasn't Mrs Hudson after all; it was our neighbours, Michael and Harry.

"Um, yeah, she's in the kitchen," I told them both, ushering them inside.

"We won't stay long, Ally. It's just that Rowan told us what your friend's been through," said Harry, dropping his voice.

Of course – Rowan and Tor had taken Tabitha back next door.

"And we wanted to give her this –" Michael held up a box of chocolates – "just to say thank you for finding Tabitha, and to cheer her up a little."

You know, they really were the nicest neighbours in the world. Their poor cat had probably got stuck in the shed after running in there to get away from Fluffy's slashing claws, but instead of holding a grudge, they were being all thankful and thoughtful.

It made me go a bit wibbly again actually. Today was turning out to be so emotional that my shirt sleeve would be soaking soon...

"Hurry up, Ro! We'll be late!" Linn's voice roared just above us, as she came thundering down the stairs. "Oh, hi, guys!"

Michael and Harry gave Linn a smile and a wave, as we all heard Rowan shout down, "I'll be there in a minute!"

"OK!" Linn yelled in reply, grabbing a jacket from the coat rail. "But I just saw Nadia parking her dad's car, so I'll meet you outside!"

"OK!" Rowan's voice drifted after her.

"Bye!" Linn waved at our neighbours and shot through the front door, leaving little old me very confused – and a very bad hostess.

"Oh, um ... just go through," I told Michael and Harry, pointing the way to the kitchen, once I remembered my manners.

I was about to follow them, when Rowan – in a whirl of colour and flying mini-braids – came charging down the stairs.

"Hey, what's going on!" I blurted out, before she sped past me.

"Oh, Ally!" gasped Ro, screeching to a halt. "It's brilliant! Linn's letting me hang out with everyone for Alfie's birthday!"

"She is?"

"Yeah! When I came home from being out with Alfie last night, she'd left a note in my room: she'd written, '*You can come out with us tomorrow if you want.*'"

"That was it?" I checked. Not exactly a grand apology for her behaviour, but I guess *any* sign of Linn thawing was good.

"Yes, *and* she was almost nice to me when we were out looking for Jen together this morning!"

A sudden noisy beep from a car horn outside made us both jump.

"Better not keep her waiting, or she'll get grouchy," Rowan winced. "But thank you, Ally – I know this is all down to you! Alfie told me last night about your idea of writing Linn a letter about how he was feeling. And it worked!"

Her braids slapped me in the face as she hugged me and she was wearing so much patchouli perfume that I nearly went giddy, but it didn't matter. The only thing that was important was that there was some kind of truce between my sisters again. And to think that I – and a couple of notes – had made that happen…

So, maybe I wasn't such a bad agony aunt, even if I hadn't been able to help Jen much. But I was only an amateur agony aunt, after all. And in Jen's

case, I had a wonderful, smart, kind mum who knew the right things to say, even if I didn't.

Right now, I wanted to run through to the kitchen and tell Mum just how wonderful and smart and kind I thought she was, but I was worried that the lump in my throat might stop the words from getting out.

Maybe I'd write it down and leave it under her pillow to find later…

HAIRY MAGGOTS RULE!

It was Monday morning, and me and my friends had five more glorious minutes of freedom till a week's worth of school started.

And what were we doing with those precious few minutes? Watching all the exchange students say their goodbyes and file on to the coach that would take them back to their small town that we'd never found out the name of.

"You know what *you* are, Ally Love, don't you!" Chloe grinned at me.

Oh, I forgot to say – my friends were also using those last, precious minutes to tease me rotten.

"I am a loser!" I said happily, caring not one tiny bit that I hadn't done The Dare, or that practically everyone on that coach knew that *I* was the girl with the loony boy mate who attacked people with ice-cream. So what? I'd never see them again. And anyway, having one of your friends go missing and turn up in your shed kind of puts everything in perspective.

Also, we were all losers in a way; after a week's worth of trailing the French visitors, we'd failed magnificently in our efforts to actually hang *out* with any of 'em. In fact, I'd got closer to hanging out with someone than my mates had, but I guess a thirty-second chat over a pig doesn't really count for much…

"*And?!*" Kyra suddenly demanded of me.

"And I'm a hairy maggot!" I announced.

"Louder!" Chloe egged me on.

"Yeah, come on, Ally!" Salma grinned. "You've got to say it louder, as punishment!"

All my friends were grinning at me, even Jen, I was pleased to see. She was standing wedged in-between Sandie and Kellie, who both had their arms firmly entwined around hers. (After yesterday's drama, none of us were going to let Jen out of our sight ever again!)

"OK!" I grinned back. "I AM A HAIRY MAGGOT!"

A few people around the playground turned to stare at me, thinking I'd gone loopy, but so what. Suddenly I felt quite giddily fearless, which was pretty unusual for a champion fretter like me.

"You know something?" Kellie giggled. "We should make Ally wear a sign that says 'Hairy maggot!' all day and – and – uh-oh … *look* who's coming over, Sandie!"

"Va-va-va voom!" Kyra murmured, as Sandie's admirer and his mate broke away from the rest of the French crew and starting walking towards us.

"Eek!" I heard Sandie give a little squeak of alarm.

Whatever SF had to say, I knew it was going to make her uncomfortable. Billy *still* hadn't made up with her after the weekend's niggling (she'd told me as much when we'd spoken on the phone last night, once we'd talked over the whole Jen situation).

"Um, hi!" SF stopped and smiled directly at my quivering best mate. "I was just thinking, I would like to have your e-mail, if that would be OK."

I didn't need to look at my other mates to know that their jaws had probably dropped to the floor right now. There was no doubting that a) SF was decidedly cute, b) him asking for Sandie's e-mail was very, *very* flattering and c) not to mention drop-dead romantic. There was only one problem, and his name was Billy. And if I knew Billy (and I did), I guessed that right now, he'd be loitering outside his own school on the other side of Ally Pally, moping like a lovesick puppy (in a baseball cap).

For Billy's sake, and for the sake of my equally

lovesick but uselessly shy pal Sandie, I had to do *something* before she ended up blurting out her e-mail address in sheer panic.

"She has a boyfriend, you know!" I butted in, stepping in between Sandie and SF.

"Oh. OK. Sorry..." he shrugged, and turned and headed back to the coach with his mate, where the last of the exchange students were shuffling on and taking their seats.

"Thanks, Ally! I didn't know how to get out of that!" Sandie sighed with relief.

"Hey, get *you*, madam!" Kyra laughed, thumping me in the arm, before I got a chance to reply to Sandie.

I supposed Kyra was as surprised as *I* was at being so bolshy all of a sudden.

"I didn't come across too rude, did I?" I asked around, instantly losing my new-found fearlessness and turning back into a flake.

"It's not *that*, Ally!" said Kyra. "I'm talking about The Dare! You finally did it!"

"When? When did I do it?"

"When you told SF that Sandie had a boyfriend!" Jen burst in enthusiastically. "You said, '*Tu sais qu'elle a déja un copain!*'"

"I did?!"

"Yeah, but I wouldn't get too excited, Ally," Kyra

smirked. "You might have done it, but you did it *last*, so you still *lost*. And you're *still* a hairy maggot!"

That got everyone laughing again, but their giggles were kind of drowned out by the roar of the coach, as it glided past us and paused at the gate, waiting for the traffic to ease.

Inside were loads of faces we'd come to recognize over the course of the week, all swivelled round as they waved at the girls and lads they'd been staying with.

Um, apart from *one* face, which was staring down at *me*...

"*Au revoir*," mouthed Stéphane, steaming up the window so that I could hardly see his smile, or the bump on his nose. But from that smile, I could tell he didn't hold a grudge against me for having an idiot pal like Billy.

"*Au revoir*..." I mouthed back silently, without my still-giggling friends even registering what was going on.

O*o-er*, I thought, as the coach juddered forward and moved off into the rush-hour Crouch End traffic. *Wonder what's French for butterflies in the stomach?*

'Cause – *zut alors!* – that was exactly what was crashing around in my tummy right then...

* * *

Anyway, that's the end of my story for today, Mum, which is good, because not only do I have a splinter in it, but my whole bum has gone to sleep from sitting on this hard wooden shed floor for so long.

How Jen managed to sleep a whole night here and not come out covered in wooden prickles and cramp I don't know. It's just as well she's back happily* sleeping in her own splinter-free bed. (*Well, OK, maybe not entirely *happily*, but things are definitely getting better for her at home, little by little, I'm v. v. glad to say.)

Well, buckets of love (as always), Mum,

Ally (* ^ _ ^ *)

PS Do you like my new smiley? It's Japanese!

PPS By the way, everything is back to slushy-gushy lovey-dovey-ness between Sandie and Billy – thanks to me. The day the exchange students left for home, I made Sandie write an e-mail to Billy. I helped her come up with it, getting her to tell him how sorry she was and how Billy didn't have to worry because it was *him* that she was crazy about, etc, etc. You know what Billy wrote back? He just wrote: (* ^ _ ^ *). Kind of cute, huh?

PPPS I found this sweet little card with a daisy on the front on my bed the other day – it was from (eek!) Alfie! He wrote to say thanks for my ace advice! Can you believe it? Of course, I was *very* cool about it, and told Rowan to tell him ta very much. What I *didn't* tell her was that I sleep with it every night and that the writing's gone fuzzy 'cause I've kissed it so many times.

PPPPS Do you think that Stéphane ever thinks about me? Y'know, maybe when he catches sight of his nose in the mirror? Or maybe when he blows it? Ah, romance!!

Make sure you keep up with the gossip!

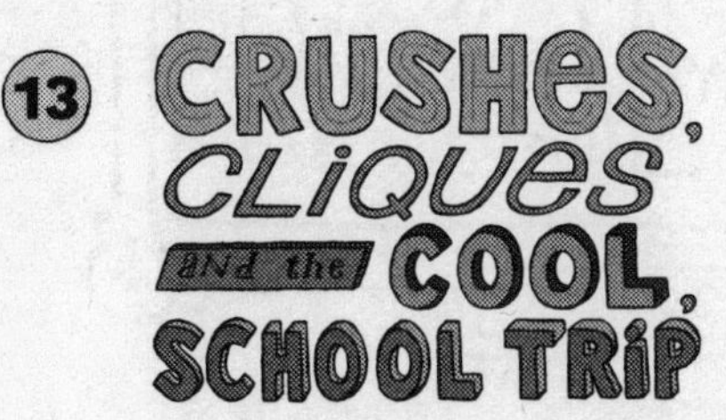

Yeah! Me and my mates are skiving school for a whole week! (Kind of...) We're all prepared for our geography field trip (apart from Kyra, who's dressed like she's going for a hike around TopShop). Only downer is, before we even get on the coach Sandie's pining miserably for Billy. But who'd have thought she'd recover so quickly...? Must be those new super new *friends* she's made for us – er, make that super new *enemies*...

Look out for loads more fab
Ally's World books!

Find out more about Ally's World at

www.karenmccombie.com

brain
full of plots, stupid stuff and cat hair
KMcC
the author

brain full of pictures, football and cat hair
the illustrator

WELCOME TO A WHOLE NEW WORLD...

STELLA ETC

FIND OUT WHO STELLA IS, MEET HER MAD TWIN BROTHERS, HER BEST MATE FRANKIE, AND A MYSTERIOUS FAT GINGER CAT...

STELLA ETC IS KAREN McCOMBIE'S SUPER-COOL NEW SERIES – IT'S FAB AND IT'S COMING SOON!